VOL 22

a collection of stories and plays

by

Dedwydd Jones

First Published in 2014 by Creative Print Publishing Ltd

Paperback ISBN 978-1-909049-29-1

Acknowledgements:

"What finally pushes us to the inaction of despair, is that we cannot protect one single being from a single moment of suffering." Ingmar Bergman

"We carry within us the wonders we seek without us; there is all Africa and her prodigies in us." Sir Thomas Browne
"May our daughters be as cornerstones, polished after the similitudes of palaces." Psalms, 144

"For us there is only the trying; the rest is not our business." TS Eliot

"The ultimate virtue is unobserved endurance." Anon

"Switzerland is a curs'd, selfish, swinish country of brutes set in the most romantic region in the world." Lord Byron

This little volume is for daughters Kelly J, Caryl J and Awen J

Once again I am greatly indebted to Maruti Morajkar for invaluable help with the computer.

Contents

CASTAWAY

A dream play in one act or so

The action takes place in the imagination

CAST

Gerald, 35, a visitor

Ceridwen, 30, Gerald's wife

Girlie, 23, Gerald's girl friend

Geoffrey, 30, his brother in law

DANIEL, Gerald's father-in-Law

1st, 2nd MAN IN MASK

Voices off stage

Chorus of masked ghouls

Parts can be doubled

(Stage hung with transparent curtains, gauzes, sound of wind blowing through them, distant thunder and lightning, a bugle calling Last Post, words of military command, echoes of distant traffic, horns, motor bikes, ambulance sirens, bombardments, collapsing buildings, distant shrieks and howls, all mixed and irregular; eerie twilight, odd shadows images flash on and off on screen, rows of phantom masks, of extraordinary hideousness, (these are to be selected from the Swiss Valley of LOTSCHENTAL'S TSCHAGGATTA Festival, see 'masks', internet) On higher level, backstage, stands GERALD, 35, strongly built, dressed in working man' clothes with gardener's belt with secateurs, boots, mobile and note book; he gazes around in awe, townscape flashes past; when Gerald 'flies' he uses his arms as a bird, whooping and dipping in mid air. He holds onto an (imaginary) boom as he mimes flying. His mobile sounds)

GERALD (Listens): O, Hello, Ma. Yes, always lovely to hear your voice. Yes, I'm on the roof of the trolley bus again, yes, number twenty-seven. No, no danger. I'm hanging on to the electronic boom, as usual. Just whizzing past the college now, where I might get a job. God, they've changed everything all round here. The wreckers with their tanks. Streets, houses, obliterated. Apt armageddons in the van. And I was only here yesterday. Listen to the bedlam, they'll never end that. Huge new block towers up to the clouds, imitation Gothic piles, gargoyles as big as your ass; new ruins on old, Jesus, what an enigma; Christ, the Coloseum just flashed past; prisons of the Fleet, execution blocks! 'Blood streams in the firmament!' Where have all the grottoes gone, the havens, bowers, rotundas, auberges, sanctums? O the folies of it all. Pardon, Ma? "And where are the ideal locations in model form?" you ask, Ma? Well, there's Avalon, the Garden of Eden, the Happy Hunting Grounds, the Land of Apples, Brigadoon, Shangri la, El Dorado and my favourite, Ma, Parnassus, the Mount of the Bards! – could be anywhere. And what is my job in all this, you ask – I am the Guardian of Lost Chords, Warden of the Golden Mean, in short Ma, I am the Chief Imagineer of the ancient Demetians! What...? Now don't worry, I'll soon have a proper job after this little adventure in foreign parts, and who knows, I might end up in the conker trees behind the old family homestead. After all I am in love with all things sylvan, dingles and copses, even down to the underbrush. No, my sleep is no longer troubled by masked succubi, I sleep like an old-born babe, really I do, I do not exaggerate, and I'll be home for the jolly hols when this is all done, I swear. Listen, Ma, this is the Guardian–Warden himself speaking. No forked tongue in sight. "Where..?"(Listens, looks around, swooping) Yes, at the traffic lights opposite the Clinic, where the girl masturbates, she's there now, so it must be Saturday morning. She is banished, you know, there is no bed for her in the family annals. They say they don't know, but I suspect. They pretend no girl whatsoever masturbates on the pavement in the centre of town, route 27, especially since the girl is from a decent family, but everyone knows she does - the jerky movements alone are a dead giveaway. Not a word against her, I try to tell them all, but they just jeer and mime wanking. Shameful. Let her alone, I cry! They cast her aside, so she does not even possess the status of a black sheep. The girl can't help it, and why not? All she's doing is what we're all doing, isn't it, trying to squeeze a bit of pleasure out of this unbelievable and bloody turmoil called life! On a common wrack, the lot of us! Bunch of wankers! (Aside) I mustn't talk to my Ma this way, must I? Yes, Ma, still on the roof, enjoying the view, wherever it is. Christ, the voices again from between the clouds, all clashing, just snatches, some boastful, some new Towers of Babel, bugger off! - can you hear the bugle call? (Listens) "Take no notice?" OK, Ma. No, Ma, me? Yes, in a dream, nor in a dream – in between. Now Ma, tell Dad this. (Reads from notebook, in broad Welsh accent) 'the Llangollen Whitebeam 'sorbus cuneifolio' is restricted to the cliffs of Eglwyseg Mountain in Dinbych, whereas in Merthyr Tydfil the motley whitebeam 'sorbus motlegiana' is really a hybred of Llew's Rowan and grows abundantly in all edgelands." Tell him. Ta , Ma, located the old herbal but yesterday. Fresh knowledge! Dad won't laugh, will he? Well, if he does, tell him this, that yesterday I had the honour of promenading at noon along the margin of a sunny field of ripening oats. Yes Ma, Quaker I imagine. That should calm him. You know what my epistemological episodes do to him. And emphasize the fact that I may be still only an apprentice tree surgeon, but with fantastic prospects, marvellous foliage, the budding historian of each and every growth of mistletoe of the old oak trees of the fucking Druids. (To audience) But in truth I know I am basically just an extremophile, survivor of the red hot lava ocean flows from the smoky vents of the earth's crust, on the midnight hour! Nothing pacific about that! Ha! *(To himself, gripping his forhead, swaying*) Damn, through the mists again, extraneous thoughts do come... "The Coelabites of the...Thespiad were assaulted by numerous naked... demons...."

*(**Yell off stage**)* : "For God's sake say something we understand!"

GERALD: 'Take no notice', as you say, Ma. Now where do I get off, how to get down? Like a swimmer of the skies, I have to swoop! The bus-stop there, by my girlie. Coming in to land! (GIRLIE in mask appears side stage. GERALD 'swims' off his perch and lands on the pavement. Smile at each other. GIRLIE has a rapid orgasm, to GERALD'S nods of approval. GERALD speaks Into mobile) Yes, Ma, I think she's come, I can see her fingers, all glistening, more relaxed too. She's nodding back to me! Lovely local vestal virgin, Ma, and all nympho, not a fake orgasm in her whole body. (Shouts) Hi, there, lovely, girl, let me tell you again - you, like me, I am proud to be associated with your frankly self-services in the open air. We, for example, constantly appear to be in a state of existence, don't we, and will anyone give us an explanation?! No, they just show us the door, so many times, before slamming it in our faces. *(Into mobile)* No, Ma, 'extremophile', that was a joke, not meant for Dad, just the leafy bits and the page numbers for him. Tell him I love the visions and that I feel so much safer up here among the vultures, you immediately know a human flesh-eater when you meet one. *(Listens. Sound of bell of 27!)* Yes, cling, cling, off you go number 27, till we ride again. Bye, bye, Girlie. You have swum into my ken again! *(GIRLIE faded off. To mobile*) OK. Love you Ma and Pa. Never not to be in touch. Promise! Cheers for the day!

1st VOICE, off stage, female, mature, screams in agony: Mother, dead! Dead! Dead! Now father, die, die, die!

(GERALD does not hear, wipes his brow, peers around, sways dizzily, pulls himself together, consults note book. Ghoul faces, masks flit, sound of sobbing, cracks of whip, grinding machinery. Image of MAN IN HOSPITAL BED, DIRTY OLD DANIEL, wrinkled, spotted, toothless, white-bearded, in hospital nightgown, torn and stained, he drools, farts, burps, splutters, scratches, spits, wanks, drinks from bedpan)

DIRTY OLD DANIEL *(Shakes fist):* I issued no orders. There wasn't a hint of evacuation there! I alone will decide when to hit the piss-pots of paradise. I gave no orders from myself alone!

(Image flickers on and off; distant music, a three-second snatch of ABBA' s 'Fernando', fade to cacophony. GERALD 'wakes' and does one or two dance steps. A smart suit in plastic Cleaner's cover on a hanger appears back stage. A figure in the gloom. GEOFFREY, 35, dressed like a bank manager, shakes the suit at Gerald)

GERALD: Where's Ceridwen?

GEOFFREY: You married a slut, didn't you?

GERALD: The forks are still dirty after she does the washing up. Not me.

GEOFFREY: You have a slut for a wife and I have a slattern for a sister, Bro.

GERALD: I am not your brother by any length of the imagination.

GEOFFREY: 'Half-brother.' Got this suit from your now sick Pa-in-law, dirty old Dan in his den of sinners - us, you, everyone, that is, this time. Better watch it, you could get blamed for everything, after all you are not from our street. Said to give this to you and not to cancel the show

GERALD: What 'show'?

GEOFFREY: The theatre one, in town or the Clinic

GERALD: But I'm not involved on stage in either.

GEOFFREY: That's what you think. *(Shakes suit)* Fresh from the Cleaner's. Gerald, dear Bro, what is this really all about?

GERALD: Drooling dirty old Dan shoved it under my very nose three months ago. "Take it!' He insisted, 'not my size,' I insisted back. The five-foot miserly dwarf! 'I can't give it away,' he goes on, 'still lots of wear in it. Your size doesn't matter, you can use it when you paint the garage walls, or do those bits in the weeds you call 'gardening' a casual labourer about the place, I suppose. It takes all sorts, as my religion says. That's where I am so lucky, I always have the right answer. But, look," he goes on, "don't you see, there's still wear in it, there, there and there. Don't put it in the bin if you don't want to. I can't deal with it, I can't rub it out, it could go on for months. You do the dirty deed yourself! The show must go on, or not, as the case may be.' Then he marches off leaving me holding the glossy three-piece. I chucked it behind a tree and fled, but he followed me and now he asks everyone to give it to me for 'the final solution.'

GEOFFREY: Every time he opens that leaden vault he calls his mouth, the trees for mile around shed their leaves.

GERALD: Reversal of nature, eh? Not bad! I didn't suspect it at first. Leave him to Lucifer, in his deadly claws. Heard they're doing tests on disgusting old him as we speak.

GEOFFREY: You know after his last by-pass op, the nurses found him in the bog having a smoke.

GERALD: What a smoke-screen is this world.

GEOFFREY: Well again, welcome Bro-in-law. My foul old half-Pa told me to say that all the time, and keep you occupied like mowing the lawn for your bread, show you round the estate, make him, that's you, Gerald, jealous of him like the rest of the human beings in the shitty toilets of the endless, farting globe. Tell him about my religion and how I dominate it, with my seraphim and cherubim, and, what's more, manipulate Lady Luck herself, by the very labia! That's me at my highest!" That's what he said. "But be cool about it, Geoffrey," he went on, "I'm in the process of making my last will and testament, but the Man-with-the- Scythe won't get me until he's got my say so, I've got some vicious connections in the heavenly pastures, so watch out, Mr Scythe! And bend the knee to your truly here, who is so much me!" Dirty old Daniel and his foetid pen, always on the lookout for a testicle or two to crush, smear a nipple ring, pull a Tampax string... I quote of course...

GERALD: ...sounds about normal for his circle of Hades.

(Image of DANIEL in hospital bed, flashes on. Goes into repulsive body noises, scratches, as at first appearance)

DANIEL: 'Normal?!' Don't count your chickens! Who am I before? Whoever I will be, I was' I was never a door without a hinge, never a soul without a sin, never a rape without a blessing, you'll be pleased to hear. To put it honestly, I am a secret agent from Heaven on direct orders from the Saviour. My personal Handler is the Archangel Gabriel himself, I hold congress with the greater and lesser prophets of all time, Moses and his bush, Abraham and his altar, etc, etc, I am not named Prophet Dirty Daniel Senior, for nothing. My task is to obfuscate all the deeper mysteries of the Bible, which sometimes, not even an owl can understand. My insights are immortalized as windows. As for you, the renewed good boys, by their own choice, go to many heavens, 77 in fact, and those who choose the evil path go to a multiplication of hells, mostly girls. The signs also lurk in ordinary things, on the pavement in black bubble gum blobs, as you wash yourself between your legs, suck your socks. How I abhor the abominations of the sycamore and the filthiness of the locust honey trees! There are endless wickednesses in gardens and allotments too, and I have been elected to recognise them at a glance, however hidden, like gooey Girlie sometimes, hidden in plain sight. I cast her out because, unlike Ceridwen, she did not confess to her multifarious sins of grunt and grind. Out, and show the world just what you are made of, I declared! And she did, like an arrow, such shame. What a film noire, threatening my bunk in Paradise, my little holy dens of gold under every dung-heap! Whereas Ceridwen was always up for it, and confessed her naughtiness to strangers in the night, and have it on from anyone, especially in the backseat of my Rolls. She recognised my exultation and gave freely. And why? Because the presence of the Second Coming is here and now and is happening all around us all over the place. You are not flesh and blood any longer, you are actually all spirit, sloughing off your sins like snakes. Ordinary things, handbags, cigarette lighters, lawn mowers all have their special spoors of good and evil, even a 'U' bend in the lavatory or wipe of the arse, have their sacred esoteric message. I know that among other chores, I am God's holy instrument for flogging by hand, as well as for bliss and manna and crab-meat, yes, the hairs in your nostrils and the wax in your ears, will not be spared. I can see it, yes, over there, stop that, sir, or I shall depress you to the seventh hell, or you madam, hands where I can see them, the Second Coming is not called that for nothing, either, and your are still under holy orders, by ME, yes, ME the mightiest of all the Serviteurs of JC, Daniel Senior, victor of all battles with the Guardian-Wardens, the so-called 'Imagineers.' Barbaric! And, yes I have to say it – jejune! Pass the word, stop casting the castaways, they're so pathetic! They will only cancel the show when I tell them in the theatre or the Green Room! As it stands, it will be all right on the night! Call the Surgeon-in-Chief, tell him to bring his sharpest scalpel, there's some tough old birds among the leathery arseholes out there tonight. Call for the Surgeon! (SCREAMS) Call for the bloody Surgeon and his scarlet fucking knife before I flat-line him with a single glance! Tell him, I'll tell him that I'll die when I like it, in theatre after theatre, cast after cast! I will give the order, me, myself, "Upstairs! Beyond the blue horizon!" Me. Upstairs! The Messiah has kicked the Archangel Gabriel off his perch so I can sit at his right hand, forever. God, I am so understanding. Eden, that's what it comes down to, all mine again, but only when I say so, and only for the likes of me, Agent Daniel Superb, Senior! Not now, not yet, not ever now or yet!

(FADE repulsive DANIEL to cacophony)

GERALD: "The show must go on or not go on," he said, the rotten old perv.

GEOFFREY:... a public show? Just a self-glorying pustule with himself centre stage, and the rest of us in our proper place, hammered shut. *(ASIDE to audience)*

GERALD: Why does no one ask about the possible contents of his will?

GEOFFREY: This location seems to get stranger and stranger, you notice that?

GERALD: Yes, even the trolley buses do not 'ding, ding' as they used to. And they've changed their number to 27 'A'. And most of the quartier has been demolished.

GEOFFREY: You don't say so?! (To audience) Heard the latest, have you? No? Well, I'll tell you – Joe Blob has fallen in love with Jenny Taylor. Geddit - Jenny Taylor…'? Laugh, go on, laugh, laugh! *(Encourages audience to laugh. Sudden hideous screech of laughter off stage. GEOFFREY immediately cowed)*

(ENTER CERIDWEN, GEOFFREY'S sister, GERALD'S wife, a sexy thirty-year old, in ultra mod gown)

CERIDWEN: Hello you two old farts.

GERALD *(Aside)* : Ceridwen, great Hag of night. *(To audience)* My wife.

CERIDWEN: That fucking suit! Why didn't you incinerate it for him?

GERALD: There was still wear in it.

GEOFFREY: Not in him, I hope.

CERIDWEN: Oh, shut up, you desicated prick.

GEOFFREY: When did you ever say 'no'?

CERIDWEN: Don't you start. Have you decided who's who yet?

GEOFFREY: What about Brendon for King Arthur?

CERIDWEN: Brendan! The guy who shambles around Aberystwyth dressed as a monk?

GEOFFREY: He was the victim of an uncontrollable nuclear fission reaction, rod overburn R.P.O. He was a top surveyor of the atomic nucleus before he became an opera singer. As a result of that dire RPO accident, he suffers from the serious distemper of impromptu laughter, of which I alone have the antidote.

GEOFFREY: And what is the antidote?

GERALD: The antidote is...there is no antidote.

VOICE *(OFF STAGE):* Fucking incomprehensible!

CERIDWEN: Why in the hell didn't you shred the threads. The Holy Father, a dismal pater, a vile groper, tell you later, might have let us stay for free in the garage garret and come up with the cash for this stupid show he's always jabbering about.

GEOFFREY: He'll put himself in the programme as both producer and director, you'll see. He'll fuck you.

CERIDWEN: Enough of you and your and Pa's primal ordure - fucking stupidity!

GERALD: True, he wanted the show to go on in the first place.

GEOFFREY: Why do you still clip his hedges and shorten his grass for him, all by yourself?

GERALD: I am the great undiscovered warden-guardian of the Demetian diplomatic corps.

GEOFFREY: Belt up, you penniless, linguistic prat.

CERIDWEN: I could have used the cellar as my boudoir. Shitty family scraps. And shopping last week, he refused to pay for the crab-meat in the shell, said I'd have to pay half of it. And there in the shop, on the counter, he divides the crab meat into two portions, in the shell, and we each paid for the his/her half. The butcher was agog. "Better than charades,' was our Pa's parting words to him.

GEOFFREY: Is the old sod dead yet? - he's had enough bloody near-death scrapes.

CERIDWEN: He's lying flat on his back in emergency, so no one can tell.

GERALD: What about Geoffrey here as Lancelot?

CERIDWEN: Bollocks! Have neither of you noticed yet that I am flowing with shiny red hair this morning?

GEOFFREY: You could do Guinevere.

CERIDWEN: That old tart!?

GERALD: Something's troubling you. Come on, out with it, no mask this time! No, on second thoughts...

CERIDWEN *(she dons a mask, in pseudo posh voice. GERALD and GEOFFREY go into tortured routines of shock/horror at the story):* Yes, your daughter here, the Marchioness of Maida Vale, turned up at the Boodles' Summer Solstice Verre Cliquot tennis party at Windrush-Bossingham Hall, and first person I saw was Princess Yasmin, with the Countess's daughter's best friend Lady Amber, and she was wearing the self same porcelain sky-blue dress as me! A downright fashion nightmare!"

GEOFFREY: Get it off your chest, Sis, that's the thing.

CERIDWEN: Leave my tits out of this, dirty old poo, too.

GERALD: In spite of his critical condition, couldn't your shite-hawk Pa give us the cash flow for the show?

CERIDWEN: He wouldn't give you the shit from under his finger nails. Hell, he's still putting it about we're staying for free in that stinking garage garret of his. So drop it, buster!

GERALD: Couldn't we put down Geoffrey here as a deposit, after all, he is a genuine step- son.

GEOFFREY: I just received this letter from the chief Surgeon, he asks us to restrain all unnecessary screams, especially the onanistic howls from the girl known as 'Girlie,' who, the Surgeon warns, is gravely threatened with all those digital agitations and is in danger of dislocating her tibia...

CERIDWEN: ...excuse me, I have to go into a toilet to laugh at a joke that shitty!

(EXIT CERIDWEN, kicking the suit ahead of her)

GERALD: 'Slut' - the understatement of the era. *(Dons a mask)* I was spontaneously chasing vagaries last night when I saw her, with her mates, reeking specialists in regurgitation, in the act of vomiting in the gutter, stuck gluttonously together like male strippers in drag, self-loathing, self pitying shrews running to fat and flatulence in well-known plazas, spoiled narcissists, foul-mouthed, immature, with piss-stained, skid-marked, sperm-soiled jokes. Later, I spotted her giving revellers 24 blow-jobs all in a row, in the market square, so much so that all the priests were alerted and had to go to the back of the queue.

CERIDWEN *(off stage, in loud whisper):* God how you must hate yourself.

GERALD: God, Jesus C, I used to love my wife, I chose her... I can't believe it. Where the fuck am I? Where have all the great cathedrals gone with their grand confessionals?

GEOFFREY: The Great Hag of Night has them in her thrall alright.

GERALD: I never suspected my ghastly Ceridwen lived in such a nest of vipers. No offense.

GEOFFREY: None taken. I should know.

GERALD: You'll inherit. He's got property all over the mediaeval City and the old countryside.

GEOFFREY: He won't cut me out. No, he can't ...he'll demote me, though, pennies not pounds, all tied up in complicated trust funds with well-paid trustees by the dozen. When he's gone, it's the lawyers for me, and I know a few ripe villains there who'll do him in, in bed or out of it. He'll die as well as decay, if I have anything to do with it!

GERALD: Everybody swears he'll survive. They blame his religion.

GEOFFREY: The fading sadist, I'll see about that.

GERALD: I wish it would rain more, it has a calming influence on the wall flowers. I'm off now, to mow a lawn or two, take in a bow or two. Ceridwen's seen dear dirty old Dan four or five times till yesterday, and she's not giving away a thing. Same for you. She won't get a bone out of him. She's keeping an eye on the whole theatre staff, in town and clinic, in case they operate on his wallet before the Xmas panto.

GEOFFREY: Cheers.

(FADE GEOFFREY. ENTER CERIDWEN, dressed in fashionable gown, waving a document)

GERALD: He's sent us a demand from his bailiffs, for three-months rent, I bet! Topsy bloody turvey turd! We've only been here three weeks.

CERIDWEN: Then do something about it. Your fault. If only you'd sent that suit away, to the salt mines, to Auswicz-BIrkenau, Hampstead, anywhere. A small thing to ask.

GERALD: Did you bring my sandwiches?

CERIDWEN: No, but I didn't forget your socks. *(Throws them at him)* And do something about that ugly cold sore on your lip. I can hardly look at you. And my boy-friends are a symptom, a trigger, not a cause.

GERALD: Trichomana vaginalis can also affect the anal cavity.

CEREDWEN: You're always peculiar after you've been thinking. Last time it was cystitis.

GERALD: The honeymooner's affliction.

CERIDWEN: Nothing to do with me.

GERALD: Passion's piss disease.

CERIDWEN: Never for the Marchioness!

GERALD: Hah!

CERIDWEN: I don't know anything about that. I'm not ashamed of my boy-friends. I was never unfaithful. I just lay there. When I'm watching TV and want a fuck, I don't go to the street for cheap pick-ups. Basically I don't want any of them But I've got a block over you. When your hand's on my belly, it's like a tarantula. And why should I deny myself the pleasures , you're older than me and done it all. You'd begrudge me a fuck with the guys who turned me on for the first time in my life. You do everything wrong as far as I'm concerned. They try every position. Buy yourself a book, yes, go out, 'How to Win Friends,' 'The Joy of Sex!' You might learn something. And I hate the curtains you chose and the forks are still dirty after the washing up...

GERALD: ...that is you!

CERIDWEN: No one helped me. I was equal to it all.

GERALD: That is not what you told me. You father...not so long ago....you're fond of telling it...go on.

CERIDEN: ...he drove me to the pine woods after the birthday party of my crazed sister and stopped in the shade of an old ash tree, leaned over to close my window, slid his hand onto my crotch and held it there, squeezing, up and down, then flipped back my skirt, ran his hand up to my cunt, which was moist already, I heartily confess it , and then with his middle finger right up, sent me to paradise, back arched in ecstasy, huge grunts, slipped off my panties, pushed me down in the back seat, I heard the zip of lust, widened my thighs, he bent over, and pushed and pushed harder, 'such little blood', he said, and up and down for forty five minutes to the second. And came I came back again and again. I had no choice, he was expiating his sin and mine too, together, intercourse was one of the Saviour's favourite signs, he said, and came all over my belly. He did the same to Ma on the same nights...

GERALD: ...regular as...go on...

CERIDWEN:... as All Bran.

GERALD: If there is a God, Jesus should have cut off his balls – right?

CERIDWEN: I didn't do it on purpose. It was such a long time ago.

GERALD: Years later, you found the Book of Family Laws open on his desk at the page on rape and incest and penalties for such, and if you'd said one word about it, he'd still be doing ten years by. And your mother…

CERIDWEN: …she didn't want to die. She yelled on her death bed, I was there, "I don't want to die. That devil will be there in hell waiting for me. I don't want to die. Die him! Die him! she cried and cried.

(Flash of DIRTY OLD DANIEL tossing, turning in hospital bed)

VOICE *(Off stage):* The nunc dimittis rehearsal now! (In plain song): 'Yes, O Lord, let your servants go in peace according to your holy word, for my eyes see the light you have prepared for all the nations and for all the glory of your true worshippers, here, corporeal, in person, never the dirty Jews, to dwell at your right hand forever, with no other soul, sprit or ghost in sight, except yours truly, here, me and myself! I alone know! After all, I have only ever taken half a dozen lives in my life, and they all deserved it! Bless you all, but much, much later."

(FADE DIRTY DAN. THE LAUGHING MAN erupts onto stage, laughing, giggling, chortling. LAUGHING MAN points into audience occasionally laughing maniacally)

LAUGHING MAN: Now who laughed that lying laughter out there then? I heard. There, there, there! You're not amused, are you, just embarrassed. There again and again. You all even laugh when I say the words, 'skid marks,' there see, not amused , or 'sperm', sperm always gets a laugh, it so leaps about the place, like shit always 'plops' about, doesn't it. I don't know – somehow too many genitalia hereabouts to night for any fun. Just piss off the lot of you, you, prime mirthless human disappointments! You can never lie to an Aphasian! Bah! You're worse than ever!

(EXIT LAUGHING MAN, the 'APHASIAN'))

GERALD: That's telling the world. *(GERALD reads)* "Marriage is just another timidity system foisted on women for sex..."

CERIDWEN: I knew it!

GERALD: Your sentiments exactly. This plan...which you assert has taken you ten thousand years to detect, is all around! Let me tell you from where I stand, men are too stupid to have thought up such a sophisticated plot, and are far too lazy to execute it.

(CERIDWEN throws a punch at GERALD. ENTER GEOFFREY)

GEOFFREY: No fisticuffs, gentles. *(CERIDWEN EXITS in a huff)* She'd do a marvellous Guinevere. But don't be too hard on her. She went to the cemetery with flowers for her grandfather's grave but yesterday, but the grave had gone, quite dug up, according to local laws, to make room for the next occupant, the skeleton dispersed, didn't leave even a finger-bone as a memento, and that's allowed, every twenty years, the time for grief over here, so she threw the flowers into the old plague pit, and still hasn't quite got over it. A bit hard to take, I must say, even for a heart of granite. The old granpa had left her strictly alone, never touched up her tities or clit, she adored him for that, and that alone.

(FADE OUT GEOFFREY. FADE IN backstage 1st, 2nd MAN IN MASKS, with judges' wigs and black cap)

1st MAN IN MASK: Kill the autopsy, your Honour, but do not mention euthanasia except in the Maker's presence. Did they plan to 'terminate' him, you ask, 'nil by mouth' him? The Nurses seemed reassuring, although one insisted that he had given her a launching party, tho' to what end no one knows exactly. And there were many visitors, visible and invisible for many thousands of terminally ill patients.

2nd MAN IN MASK: So, you heard, your Honour?

1st MAN IN MASK: Many times.

2nd Man: The mourners were there.

1st MAN IN MASK: But no question of tears.

2nd MAN IN MASK: He was terminated.

1st MAN IN MASK: By whom.

2nd MAN IN MASK: By himself.

1st MAN IN MASK: Which one?

2nd MAN IN MASK: The one in the mirror.

1st MAN IN MASK: What about a period of grief, your Honour?

2nd MAN IN MASK: He'd just had one, your Honour.

1st MAN IN MASK: Did you go and visit him?

2nd MAN: I did indeed.

1st MAN IN MASK: Day or night?

2nd MAN IN MASK: Backwards and forwards.

1st MAN IN MASK: Cherchez la femme?

2nd MAN IN MASK: Your Honour?

1st MAN IN MASK: Yes, your Honour?

2nd MAN IN MASK: Christ, you are so fucking ugly!

1st MAN IN MASK: Watch it, buddy!

2nd MAN IN MASK: Look, like I was telling you, your Honour, I left Beth and took up with Lucy, so cheerful but she couldn't cook and she a West Indian. You like black girls? Yes, white is best, nothing like one, all lily-white, like swans. Lovely. But Lucy...Women, always want something, money, see, sex, romance, 'After Eights.' Well after what happened with Lucy, all women are deadwood to me now, deadwood! Know what happened, we were having a drink in the pub, me and Lucy. Mac came in, he'd had his eye on her, he just marched across to her, went on his knees, and said, "I love you, Lucy. Marry me!" She got up, hugged him and said "Yes, yes, yes!" and they both left of the Registry Office. That was the end of that. I tell you, women, all deadwood now.

1st MAN IN MASK: 'Cept Girlie.

2nd Man IN MASK: 'Cept Girlie.

(FADE 1st, 2nd MAN IN MASKS. ENTER CERIDWEN, GERALD)

GERALD: I tell you, when I woke up this morning, there was a wonderful tree in the garden.

CERIDWEN: You do not say.

GERALD: I take great comfort in the continuance of the Douglas Fir.

CERIDWEN: Who the fuck killed cock-robin? He was breathless and hateful when last I saw him. In that condition, he only had hours to go. And you?

GERALD: Same. *(Consults note-book):* Let me tell you now of the plant 'uva ursi', now this one has many anti-septic properties, by virtue of a gloyoside known as arbutin. This is absorbed by the body and broken down into hydroquinine and glucose. When the hydroquinine is excreted, it exerts a benign antiseptic action on both kidney and bladder, but your urine has to be alkaline, so be sure to eat plenty of fresh fruit.

CERIDWEN: Well, there you go.

GERALD: Who do you think is finally going to do the old swine in?

CERIDWEN: We were a happy united family, you know, especially from the outside, he made sure of that.

GERALD: His arteries were clogged with tar, his lungs rotted with nicotine, his mind deranged with God.

CERIDWEN: Rumours! Kids' stories!

GERALD: From the exterior only. Did you question the surgeon-in-Chief?

CERIDWEN: In his very theatre, no one escapes.

GERALD: Who authorized the certificate?

GERALD: Death.

CERIDWEN: What a wicked thing to say.

GERALD: Just trying to keep in touch with my feminine side.

CERIDWEN: Pardon?

(Consults note-book)

GERALD *(Reads)* : 'Anima', the dominant household being, is the female essence or directive which flits around the subconscious ambiance of the home...'

CERIDWEN: ...when I was out shopping yesterday, I saw a row of flower pots outside the shop, "Ideal for graves," the assistant said, making the sign of the cross, but I didn't believe a word of it.

GERALD: When did you last hear your sister scream?

CERIDWEN: Don't look at me.

GERALD: How agèd are you, Ceridwen?

CERIDWEN: For my last birthday, I got champagne and – thrush, fuck it!

GERALD: Look, ignore the drunken kangaroos and the weeping nuns, you're right, the key to the secret of life lies somewhere under the toilet bowl. (Consults note-book) I feel I'm on an endless wrecked, merry-go-round loaded with the uneasy, unfamiliar corpses of all the ages I have never known. How in the hell can you feel sorry for everyone if you live next door to a graveyard? Did you know beehives are said to be the final retreats of departed spirits - while all the time, what we search for so heartbreakingly is for just little golden corner, in nature or in human nature, where we can sit and muse and drink every day with no hangover. A little golden corner. That's all. (Reads) "...the interlockings of knowledge, the objective correlative, come from familiar feelings of finality, and the actualisation of their inchoate nature - then, and only then, will the post duende beacons of truth shine out...'

CERIDWEN *(Mimes pulling chain):* All your bloody useless jaw should be heard to the sound of toilets flushing, there's so much shit in it.

(Sound of genuine loud laughter)

GERALD *(Reading):* 'To us sons of exhortation, religions, Moses, eg., are merely history distorted between layers of false language. You must burrow between these obscene layers of lies and you will discover the Mysteries , the real repositories of human truth.'

CERIDWEN: Did you get that useless idiot's job at the College Geoffrey arranged?

GERALD: 'Come back when you're famous, come back when you're dead, come back when the moon is a glorious red.' *(CERIDWEN mimes pulling chain)* No. But I will never be guilty of the sin of worldly sorrow. Totus mundus agit histrionem. What does that vulgate mean, you ask. It was a sign up outside the Globe Theatre, and it means 'we're all players.'

CERIDWEN: Darkness and Diarrhoea, we have this tragedy on our doorstep and all you do is talk in filthy riddles and disgusting innuendo, you douch bag!

GERALD: And for your birthday, did I not create for you an enchanted dream world, it opened with a glistening red apple, remember, hanging over the head of a bust of Sir Isaac Newton, with a sequined fox looking out from a cabinet of curiosities, as a child whispers nursery rhymes from inside the wax-work model of the life-size palace bog. And when the sickly boy prince, who kept a feral urchin as a pet, died, London ran out of black mourning crepe...'

VOICE *(Screaming)* : Let him die. Now! Now.

CERIDWEN: He is fucking good as dead, you cretine, we're on the whodunnit and who-gets-the-dosh bit now, so ease your stupid joints and piss off with your silly screams. *(SCREAMS CUT ABRUPTLY)* You count your curses, I'll count my blessings, lovers, husbands, even thrush made me think. He did it in the backwoods, dirty toad. At only nine, I learned as much as twenty harlots a night, a sin forgiven every second, he said. God, I was brought up behind my back, so I never knew what was going on, and they knew that. And now I've got too many dicey tastes to stop one inch of it.

(FADE OFF CERIDWEN. FADE ON GIRLIE)

GIRLIE: When dirty old Daniel tried it out on me, I screamed his name a thousand times in the specious streets until and he had me sectioned, which was exactly my plan for getting out of that infested sty of a house, and I've been doing my five-finger exercises vigorously on Saturdays ever since, to ensure my little retreat in paradise kindly stayed where it was, in the mad house. They left me alone to rot, but actually I was left alone to live. You should see my encyclopaedias and DVD's, so many friends, like the Laughing Man, my sole Aphasian, truth-teller, then my disembodied voices, Fernando, allies and all so heedless, without a single belladonna or a garrote as far as eye can see. Friends that fly to you like that please the heavens. But no one noticed me, except you, dear Gerald, thank God, Gerald, all in a half-dream, you said. True?

(FADE ON DIRTY OLD DANIEL in hospital bed, surrounded by machines bleeping, tubes, drips on stands, attached to his body. Mutters, shakes fist, gives orders, masturbates, stops, frustrated. Cacophony of sounds, as at beginning. GEOFFREY, CERIDWEN appear out of shades, approach DANIEL, hands stretched out like claws, they reach for him, fiend-like)

DANIEL: *God, no! I gave no orders. No... no...not yet! No...no...*

(Sound of tram, 'ting a ling,' general cacophony as long as fight lasts. CERIDWEN, GEOFFREY swoop down on dirty old DANIEL. DANIEL fights them of. As they tear at the tubes, DANIEL hangs on to the tubes, tug of war, tubes snap; DANIEL threshes about, tearing down tubes and wires. They tear off DANIEL'S gown, slash his body, beat, hammer his head, hurl him to the floor, stamp him to death. DANIEL is still. FADE. The gory panorama FADES with CERIDWEN, and GEOFFREY still stomping. 1st

and 2nd MASKS and GERALD fade on. (Masked VOICES (also in judges' wigs) 'interrogate' GERALD)

1st MAN IN MASK: So you went to see him then?

2nd MAN IN MASK: I went to see him, yes, your Honour.

1st MAN IN MASK: And the lady known as 'Girlie'?

GERALD: Yes, your Honour, she went to see him too.

2nd MAN IN MASK: You were mowing the grass outside as an employee, Girlie was moaning and groaning, as a relative inside, so you didn't have to sign the visitors' book.

1st MAN IN MASK: So there is no evidence that you were really there.

2nd MAN IN MASK: Spot on, you Honour. None of us were really there.

1st MAN IN MASK: Did you see Ceridwen?

GERALD: She was alone with Daniel for a while.

2nd MAN IN MASK: Did you see Geoffrey?

GERALD: He was alone for a time with Daniel too.

2nd MAN IN MASK: Did you know about Ceridwen and Daniel?

GERALD: Ceridwen told me.

1st MAN IN MASK: And Ceridwen and Geoffrey?

GERALD: The one thing I hoped would never be fact, your Honour.

2nd MAN IN MASK: Did you tell Girlie all this?

GERALD: No.

1st MAN IN MASK: Why not?

GERALD: She knew already.

2nd MAN IN MASK: What have you to say in your defiance?

GERALD: Ceridwen, Geoffrey, Daniel, the Holy Trinity – the final solution, there you have it! 1st MAN IN MASK: At last!

2nd MAN IN MASK: I think that is more than enough, *(Bangs gavel)* The guilty are over there!

1st MAN IN MASK: But Gerald, what was dirty old Daniel's point? Why did he drag it out for so long?

GERALD: If I may venture a last word, your Honours - the unspeakable Daniel wanted to breathe one more time in order to commit one last blast, one full, final fell black order - like - 'Fall out the maggots! Fall in the sinners! We in the end are the glorious winners"" What are the two nutters up to now?

1st MAN IN MASK: Ceridwen and Geoffrey are in illegal congress, and have hired a battery of lawyers behind them – they have decided it's all dirty old Daniel's money in their grimy palms, or their own deaths on the line. They've cleared up the mess at the hospital, concealed the evidence, the remains are decently interred already, no bones about it. They've set up home in Daniel's former bedroom and adjoining chambers. They have each other again, in bed and out of it, till nil-by-mouth doth them part, they think. They said you could now stay out late without their permission, to take your gardening tools with you – and - fuck you - generally!

(FADE OUT 1st, 2nd MAN IN MASK. FADE OUT GERALD. FADE ON GIRLIE. Fade on GERALD, 'flies' down to join GIRLIE)

GERALD *(Bowing):* Your very own favourite Imagineer has returned.

GIRLIE: Straight from King Arthur's Court, no doubt.

GERALD: I played all the parts. I am guiltless on every count.

GIRLIE: Of course you are. They are my friends after all said and done.

GERALD: Semper fi!

GIRLIE: So I am very glad to see my darling extremophile back this Saturday morn, and looking so cool.

GERALD: And I didn't forget the mistletoe, I promise. Carry on.

GIRLIE: I'm being shown the door as well, aren't I?

GERALD: Slammed shut again, thank god.

GIRLIE: Still with no explanation for our existence.

GERALD: Yes. And you?

GIRLIE: Are you going home?

GERALD: No.

GIRLIE: Why not?

GERALD: Ma, Dad, I love them too much.

GIRLIE: What are you going to do then?

(GERALD spreads out his arms to her. Cacophony up as at beginning; fades, sound of ABBA's 'Fernando' song, just a few bars; GERALD takes GIRLIE's hand, they embrace, begin dancing to 'Fernando', a few bars only. Dance into the shadows, a loving couple, gazing into each other's

eyes. Cut lights, music up with house lights, 'Fernando' again as audience exit)

CURTAIN

No Stones Unturned

"The directions from the twins were quite clear," said Beryl, "to kick off this glorious day with the Stone Skimming Competition. Right here! So come on!"

Barry and Beryl, well into their fifties, stood on the shale and pebbles of the river bank, selected the flattest stones at their feet, paused, aimed, then hurled them across the lapping waters. Barry's skipped once, twice, thrice. Beryl's jumped once, twice, thrice and a fourth time. Beryl had won. She punched the air and pranced around.

"My hit, first blood," she shouted and waved, "one, nil! Let the twins see that!"

"How do you know they're watching?" asked Barry, casting a look over the hill rising behind them.

"I bet they're up there with their big binoculars, the sly boots, so let's put on a show!"

"What've we let ourselves in for, following the twins' mad clues to the bitter end," he muttered, more to himself than Beryl. "Crazy!"

A faint hooting sound carried across the river from the weeping willows.

"Listen, was that an owl?"

"That was a dove, love, silly boy! Now, just follow orders, Barry, play the game - we've got to leap-frog to the old style, find the next clue, then up and beyond the cairn at the top of the hill. Another one there. And so on! So move, my man, move!"

"Charge!" yelled Barry. Beryl promptly bent down and Barry vaulted over her raised backside. Then it was Barry's turn. This they repeated until they were up to the old wooden style, as instructed by their own kids, boy and girl, Jan and Jim, twenty and twenty, identical twins –

their parents' twenty-fifth wedding anniversary, right in the middle of these parts!

Beryl flopped down by the style. The race had nearly broken her heart and had almost done for Barry too. He had won by a gasp but was now sweating like a landed athlete in the shade of the hedge. Below them spread a bright and sparkling meadow running down to the waters of the river and the drooping willow trees. The stream glided slowly onwards to the distant sea, through rich, lush pastures, spread with buttercups, daisies, and poppies and acres of ladies' bedstraw. The meadow stood next to the cultivated orchard-garden of the Drapers' Arms, the biggest pub for miles, everyone's favourite, the tables always overrun with Granny Smiths and rosy pippins for the picking, the centre of the cider trade in the area. They took in the sweeping view with nostalgia. The slopes were alive with the sound of drinking – it was the day of the annual races, and the splendid Applefest and Cider Fete of a really special anniversary, and everyone knew it! The hill was crawling with celebrating neighbours and curious onlookers.

"Just like when we were kids," mused Beryl, back to her old self, indicating the whole area with a sweep of the hand

"No," responded Barry, "I used to win every time."

"Leap-frogging uphill," said Beryl with a laugh, "that really is for kids!"

"No. For our anniversary."

"Age - the worst obstacle-race of all!" said Beryl, "but it can be funny, can't it?"

"Twenty-five years, and still going strong - just!"

"We've got to find that next one," said Beryl, "and no excuses, in spite of the fact we're hitting over half a century."

“What a way to celebrate our sweet years together - set up by our own kids! I said!” Barry gave his wife a smacking kiss. She pushed his hand off her buttock but let him put it back. They poked around in the tufts of grass and under the slats of the style.

“What’s this?” Barry picked up a scrunched up ball of coloured paper, about to discard it.

“Give it here, Barry, you’re no good at clues. Look!”

She smoothed out the paper. In the palm of her hand lay a stone, a simple stone, round, brown and nondescript.

“That’s nothing,” said Barry, “chuck the thing into the deep end!”

“Not while we’re still celebrating. Now watch.”

She eased out the wrinkles and read the place names on the fragment, “see, it’s a part of one of those ordinance survey maps...”

“Why,” said Barry excitedly, “ it’s us, I mean, look there, our home, the Draper’s Arms, pub and orchard, Greenman Wood, the whole Fete in the far field by the Drapers’, Oldings’ Farm for fresh eggs, the Cider Press for fresh booze, the Dairy for babies’ milk, the Ouse Jetty for the flotilla, and, look, the style’s marked with a cross, here; there, the next stone, up here at the cairn. “ He paused, scratching his head, “here, any of these spots remind you of anything...?”

“...No! Now jump to it!”

“We don’t have to leap-frog again, do we?”

“Come on, get on with it,” Beryl urged, “no slacking, the twins would never forgive us, in front of the neighbours too, and from even farther off, strangers!”

When they reached the summit, Beryl felt her head whirling, Barry felt a strong urge to retire. They both paused for breath. Beryl finally waved the scrap of paper under Barry’s nose.

"This is a very precious bit of map! It tells us how old we are without ageing us!" She put it carefully into her pocket. "Come on, Barry, never mind the dizzies, we'll call that a draw, we've got to celebrate. On with the show! "Now," she went on, "more stones. Turn them over. Leave not one stone unturned. And take your hand off my bum!"

"But don't you remember - here, I mean..."

"...that's all you ever think of, isn't it?"

"It would be worse if I didn't!"

"Big deal! Get going, and no fooling around this time!"

Barry staggered to his feet and promptly tripped the pile over and fell sprawling! But there it lay, the next stone-with-a-message, exposed - quite deliberately it seemed, concealed under tufts if grass. Beryl hurriedly unwrapped it, a bit of quartz, quite ordinary, really, but this time there was no mistaking, she flattened out the fragment of map, and pointed, the route was traced in red, to the next stop - "to the Earth Worm Competition" Beryl read out loud. She pointed towards the field of the fete in behind the pub.

"Remember when we were courting - seventeen or eighteen, was it, Barry? Who won then? Come on, a sentimental journey, all planned by our kidoes!"

"It's a trap, I tell you!"

"It just isn't, I tell you!"

The jousting ground had been carefully prepared. The tall Umpire-in-chief was ready for the next labour and beckoned frantically to the puffed-out couple to get inside the arena, and join in. The place of combat was roped off, about the size of a cricket pitch. On this space were numerous human beings behaving very oddly - all on their hands and knees, hammering the soil, sometimes with their fists, or the flats of their hands, stamping, treading, crunching down or using discarded boards, all slapping mother earth as if she had committed some terrible crime. Sudden cries of astonishment and cheers of joy rose into the air. The slappers paused, staring downwards at the spaces in front of them. The tall Umpire now hurried over and began inspecting the patches which were now a mass of writhing earthworms, all alive and well, frantically moving in search of the rain - it had to be near, the worms had all heard the sound of the torrents hammering on the surface soil, so the refreshing liquid was bound to be close. The tall Umpire began counting up each individual pile of worms, making a careful note of the names and numbers. It was at this point that Beryl moved in for the kill – with a cur-like bark, she leaped into her rapid pounding, yelping war dance of the complete Apache nation. She struck the earth like a demented Indian brave warming up for a sortee against the entire US cavalry! The tall Umpire paused, stock-still, staring at Beryl's lightning feet, shook his head in amazement and began the last count. He moved among the other more subdued turf warriors, then turned and shouted to the crowd, "Yes, our Beryl here, on her anniversary, with her consort King Bean, by her side, has won the annual Earthworm Competition, and it was close, I can tell you, - by one worm! Thirty-one to thirty-two."

The onlookers cheered wildly. The tall Umpire ecorted the couple, victor and vanquished, to the prize-giving podium. On it, right in the centre, awaited the next paper-wrapped stone, still a bit more of their own territory, they now knew - whichever way they turned, it was home, all the old familiar places! Marvellous! Yes, Beryl was right, the twins had excelled themselves, but for the moment were keeping well out of the way. They had promised 'something plain and simple!' But this was a feast and a fete of fun and must have cost a bomb. The twins were now the toast of the neighbourhood. Yes, everyone saw that the Happy Couple had accumulated enough events to last a lifetime, the kids had proved it, the little monkeys!

Beryl handed the piece of map to the tall Umpire, who announced, "Now to our village's ancient Gothic Competition, 'the Gargoyle Yell!'" The Man here has 'to howl the apple', the lady has 'to grin the cake!'" -

the most fiendish, wins!" He placed a splendid granny apple on the table, followed by a most sumptuous eight pound fruit cake. The opponents kissed each other and faced the music. Barry opened wide his mouth and uttered the most dreadful howl he could think of - enough to inter the living let alone raise the dead! - but it wasn't enough to move the shining pomme. Beryl now prayed, 'for God's sake, let me grin from the heart!' and took up her worm-charmer's stance, glanced sideways at the apple like a flirt in a Spring fling, and gave a great spreading warm Chesire cat kinda thrillin' grin, which ran way down the very middle of the cake and spread out far over the throng like a sweet Spring shower. The grinning-cake had indeed travelled far and wide, easily outdistancing the vulpine howl of Barry. More definite cheers for Beryl! There was little doubt, she had won the over-arching anniversary prize. The score, three to Beryl, two to Barry, with the whole world waiting for the climax. Behind the tent, the naughty twins chuckled and clapped although they had been paralyzed with embarrassment by the cavortings of their parents. Never mind, the map was working wonders, and 'we were all young once' thought the Happy Couple. And Barry sagely added, 'if this is all behind us, imagine what there is to come!"

The Umpire now rolled the stone to the Happy Couple. Beryl unwrapped it and gasped – this was a ripe one!

"The frog-hopping race has come and gone," declared the Umpire from his great height, "but the slow one lies ahead. I give you all, on this anniversary day, the Slowest Race of Man!" He held up his hand. "A brief historical note first, this race was originated by Phoenician traders to honour their great God, Baal. Thank you."

'Heck, how did we say OK to all this?" thought Barry. 'The Slow Race,' he remembered from his youth, was the most strenuous race of all. Over the top! The tall Umpire, now silent again, measured out the finishing line and hung up the tape. He positioned the Happy Couple on the far side of the tape with their backs to it, facing in the 'wrong' direction. The aim was to move backwards for four paces as slowly as possible, and whoever arrived last, was first. Simples really, though Beryl, she had never won this race during their young days and was determined to be number one at last! She stiffened her sinews and moved as imperceptibly as a snail, the movements of her arms and legs were so infinitesimal that Barry thought she had had a seizure. Barry saw at once that he was being undertaken, and steadied his resolve, but too much, leaning forward by that half an inch, he found he could not stop - he rolled onto the ground in slow motion, backwards into the dreaded tape, with a bellow of animal despair! Beryl flung her hands up and punched the air – the ladygirlwifemotherlover was Championne this time, the slowest woman in the world! After a brief breather, the tall Umpire dived down into the disturbed earth and came up with the next stone. He unfurled it. It was, yes, 'the Oarless Coracle Race,' he announced, "down by the riverside!" Barry knew this one. They marched down to the bank where two coracles, bereft of oars, were moored. The Umpire Chief held them fast until Barry and missus were settled in. With a shove, the he pushed them out into deeper waters, spinning like tops. As soon as Barry began seeing fish, he knew what to do. He saw Beryl was regretting the day she was born, and was whizzing around again so she couldn't remember or make out, a thing. Barry stood to attention, saluted like a martinet, threw a kiss to his missus - and leaped overboard. He reached up, gripped the side of the coracle and kicked out, towing the odd vessel to shore. A life-boat had to be sent for poor Beryl. As soon as she was settled again, and the scores equal, the looming Earth Worm Umpire announced the next turn of events.

"And now, not a few feet away, I give you the Bog Snorkling Relay! Follow me to the soggy wetfields of the Anniversary!" He marched off, followed by the entire crowd, neighbours and strangers, drunks and piss-takers, down to the river's edge.

"I'll get you this time," hissed Beryl aside, with a kiss, "you shall not pass!"

The equipment lay ready on the site, the streaked, purplish stretch of bog marked out, twenty yards of murky depths. The tall Umpire checked their gear, helped them to dress, lined them up on the side of the reeking morass and shoved them in. There was no splash, just a sort of sinister gurgle. They both made with the breast stroke, but got so tangled in the bog-weed they froze to a halt, their legs flailing as if in chains. At that moment, they both raised their arms in defeat. Not only were they blinded, they were winded as well. The tall Umpire and the Assistant Umpires dredged them out and washed them down. The tall Umpire declared it was no race due to the weather and led them up the garden path back to the Slow Race podium to reveal the next station of their heavy cross. Hearty cheers urged them on. What a couple, still with a smile on their faces - but murder in their hearts for the terrible twins. But who was to know that, and did it really matter? The tables were now covered with jars and pots and buckets of flowers - carnations, dahlias, chrisanthemums, jeums, cosmoses, even tons of the strikingly humble wall flowers for everyone.

"And now..." the towering Umpire thundered on, "the Floral and Foliage Ceremonies, one hundred per cent unique to this area! – the enshrinement of Mother Flora and the Green Man! - the last lap of this tremendous anniversary ensemble!"

"What a bash! What a bash!" the spectators enthusiastically shouted now and again. The twins doubled up with mirth behind the tent and sneaked off down to the river-going vessel to take their allotted place on the bridge of time, and reveal the final passage of the odd and charmful odyssey.

The tall Umpire now unwrapped the last of the stones and hurled it into the crowd. "Do your most green and floral thing!" he yelled. More cheers. The audience now pushed forward and surrounded the tables. They plucked up all the blossoms, and using the safety pins so thoughtfully provided by the establishment, proceeded to pin the blossoms over every inch of the bodies of Beryl and Barry, until they were practically invisible to the human eye. The wall flowers were especially noticeable, being the brown crown that hung over their eyes, so not even a sniper could get at them. When the Happy Couple groped forward to sing the usual song, the Umpire halted them, declared them eternally drawn, forever blessed in the race of one sex against the other, and pointed down towards the river. Yes, out of the huge hanging branches of the willows on the far bank, the stately old narrow boat appeared, pushing the dangling foliage aside, re-painted, re-furbished for the occasion, as if decked out for a royal garden party, as if riding on a cushion of warm, country air. The twins, Jim and Jan, stood at the helm, the wheel in their hands, their pet owl on his perch on the roof. 'Hoot, hoot' came the hollow, fluttering, familiar, kindly call. Even as Barry and Beryl waved and hooted back, the twins unfurled the narrow boat flag, out it fluttered - the entire map of the region revealed in silk, but without the gaps to show the stops, just the whole homestead, clean and bright, untarnished, untorn, indeed, almost pristine! The flag streamed proudly in the heedless summer breeze over the noble Ouse; and every stop for a clue, every pause for a stone, had been genuine, every shady nook authenticated, for these spots were where both Beryl and Barry had shagged in the old days and nights of their youth, of precious memory which the entire community approved of, as they now showed. The prow of the boat hoved into full view; on it, in Gothic lettering, was its new name, the 'Beryl and Barry!' both of whom, in some astonishment, now prepared to mount their wonderful repainted narrow boat, the spectators applauding and slapping the many-coloured floral couple on the back - their multiple couplings known and revered by all, and this very last stop, the narrow boat now tied up at the jetty, was where they had spent their honeymoon, where the twins had been so tenderly conceived. A mighty 'hurrah' went up from the villagers, as the couple mounted the gang-plank, embraced their laughing, treasured offspring, saluted the last spot of the of their championship matings, all known by heart, the peoples' favourite, the Happy Couple, Barry and Beryl, who never left one stone unturned. “Hoot, hoot” went the owl, wiser than all the failings of man, as the Floral Lady and the Green Man reached the end of their particular little anniversary pilgrimage and settled down in the snug of the night for some more - or so it was said!

Happy Birthdays

Cliff climbed out of the taxi in the parking place of the Maternity Unit, paid the driver and walked reluctantly to the main entrance. The night-light was on already. Gloomy black clouds billowed in the shadows of the surrounding hills, ready to change the twilit scene into dark night.

What a time to have baby, he thought. He hoped Mary was OK, she'd caught the infection the day she came in, and had to get over it before they could induce labour. She'd been here for almost four days now. The doctor had been quite honest. To Cliff's question, he had replied, "Yes, the infection was due to the abortion, however long ago it was, but it should clear up, it's her first and that's proving difficult for her. But she'll be all right. Ring Reception when you want." That damn abortion. Wasn't his, or hers, for that matter. A one- night stand when pissed with a perfect stranger. Another penalty for having been born, no doubt. Mary was twenty, he thirty; she, a student finishing her degree; he a supply teacher dying to get out of the profession, so many people a day, so many packed classes, too much sweat and blood, like here, he thought.

He pushed the door open and approached the Receptionists' counter. Sally, the friendly, helpful trainee nurse, still a little too young for disillusion, was at her desk, fresh-complexioned, and instantly appealing. But Sally was learning fast and cast a leery eye whenever Head Theatre Sister Annie Smith, appeared. Sister Annie had become her number one managerial pest. Behind young Sally, fixed onto mobile screens, were a myriad drawings from the Nursery Ward - wildly coloured, weirdly shaped, vividly imaginative. But each drawing was placed geometrically in line smothering any spontaneity in the images. Theatre Sister Annie's hard orderly hand was never far off. Below the last daub, next to the desk, the most important pronouncement was printed – 'Exhibition curated by Head Theatre Sister Annie Smith!' The lettering was larger than the drawings. Sally caught Cliff's glance.

"All Theatre Sister's Annie's," Sally remarked with a shrug, "on the high road to

International success. Right now! And I've got another pile here to pin up too," she went on, "and the Hospital magazine's going to do an article, and the local Press's coming for pictures."

"Busy little bee," Cliff said, remembering the hatchet face, the smile of a crocodile, the cold glaucous gaze of a stick creature, the chilling sound of a rattler in the night – Cliff couldn't help mixing his beasties - for Head Theatre Sister Annie Smith really was an amalgam of nasty insects, reptiles and instruments of torture.

A wide strip of cardboard hung high above the impromptu gallery, 'You are now entering the House of Good Cheer!' it read, "do not forget to Smile!" with a grinning little manikin below.

"She told me to put her name on every sheet," said Sally shaking her head, "and pin up more to fill any spaces, and to draw them myself if there wasn't enough room. And with thanks for that, she gives me night duty for weeks. Well, tonight I'm staying out, whatever. And look at that silly notice, 'Welcome to our House of Good Cheer,' – you know, she orders us all to say that to visitors however often they've visited. Stupid." In a parody of Sister Annie, she shouted out like an army drill instructor, "Platoon – House of Good Cheer – salute!" She saluted. "Like that! All that row for damn Mistress Big-Head-Smith!"

Sudden distressful noises echoed down the corridor behind Sally. "Damn! Evening Family Feed again," Cliff said, "I forgot." This was the part he hated. Waves of mindless baby shrieks greeted him, muted, gargling howls, all still objecting to the sight of the frightful human day no doubt - all mingled with sounds of hurrying footsteps, the swish of automatic doors, the clatter of crockery and steel instruments on metal trays. Then the stench hit him. It surprised him every time. Shit, piss, halitosis, farts, sputum, sweat, baby phlegm, so strong he longed for the familiar pong of disinfectant. What a messy business birth is, he thought, or is it just life? Sally wrinkled her nose and Cliff quailed as the sounds engulfed them. Before the visitors arrived en masse for the supper show, the two adopted a formal vein, a self-defensive formula to put off all boarders.

"Good evening, Trainee Nurse Sally," said Cliff, raising an imaginary hat.

"Evenin' Mr Roberts," Sally responded with a toothpaste laugh - a gay little sound, and perfectly meaningless - as it was meant to be. Cliff bowed. They had both gone up in the world.

"And how's my wife Mrs Mary Roberts, trainee Nurse Sally?"

"No change, sir. Head Theatre Sister Annie said she was sleeping. "

"In spite of Head Theatre Sister Annie, I thought I'd wait here for a while, just in case."

"Head Theatre Sister Annie said your wife just had a bad day, that's all, sir. "

"I heard my wife yelling from A Block when I came in last night."

"That wasn't her, sir," Sally replied, "Theatre Sister Annie said a whole lot of emergency births all of a sudden..."

"...but, nice trainee Nurse Sally, my wife is in the emergency ward..."

"...it's just more convenient, sir, she said."

"Is it?"

Sally suddenly pointed. "There! Talk of the devil, Sister Annie! Look!"

Cliff turned in time to glimpse the gorgon striding down the corridor, push her way through Surgery's plastic swing doors, her tight green plastic apron still running with rivulets of blood, and rip off her surgical gloves before she disappeared. Please no. He shut his eyes and swayed. But he hadn't fainted yet as some of the fathers had. Head Theatre Sister Annie had no belief in man, and even less in women. Her fixed aim was to give self- promotional orders at every opportunity in every department, even if they involved death sentences. She pecked away at the infected dust in the barnyards of life, the equal of any cock-crow on the dung heap of the world, and she always came out on top, as she would in this particular 'House of Good Cheer', she was determined. The only thing that mattered was that the diktats worked.

As the chattering visitors began to drift in, Cliff prayed for it to be over soon, especially for dear, defenceless Mary.

"I'll let you know," said Sally, smiling reassuringly, reading his thoughts. "It'll be alright."

"You're real nurse already, Sal. See you later."

He made his way to the visitors' waiting room, the shabbiest space in the Happy Home. The sofa and three arm chairs were worn to their wooden frames, the cushions were threadbare and the solitary table loaded with out-of-date magazines. The curtains sagged as if about to tumble to the floor. Cliff's spirits drooped immediately. He did one depressing turn of the room and stepped back into the corridor. Time to check Mary in the emergency ward. He tip-toed inside with trepidation. At once he was greeted by a chorus of groanings, heavy breathings, hissings, shiftings, the occasional abrupt shriek, which made him jump, all emanating from the six beds with their bulging, ceaselessly uneasy occupants, still incapable of giving that final push to birthright and daylight. He looked down at Mary. As Sally had told him, Mary was asleep. Her face was taut and glistened with a sheen of sweat, her blond hair plastered across her face. He smoothed the damp locks aside, ignoring the huge lump below her navel. Let it be over, he begged again. Mary moaned faintly, giving a strange double jerk from time to time, as if in the middle of a nightmare, which, of course, she was. The patient in the next bed raised herself up on her elbow, and motioned towards Mary.

"Hello, Kate," Cliff muttered, dying to escape the small suffering hell of a cell. He had got to know Kate and her husband, Tom, during his trips to the hospital. Kate was a shop assistant in Boots and was rising in the Chemists' hierarchy. She was Cardiff born and had a broad Cardiff accent. Her husband Tom was an engineer, as he described it, but 'highway labourer' better fitted the situation. He hailed from Pontypridd, his present place of abode, better known as the Township of Tom Jones. He believed Kate had married above her station and that he had married below it. They had one other child, a girl, at present being cared for by Kate's sister. They lived on the outskirts of the town. Kate beckoned to Cliff confidentially, "Listen, I know what's going on, I've been here before. Mary shouldn't be in here, it's her first, and the others are shouting and groaning all night. Their meds don't make any difference. Mary hasn't had a chance to sleep. This is the first time she's slept for two days. She's getting weaker, two of the women here won't make it outside. Help Mary out of here, Cliff. Get jumped up Sister bloody Annie, the bitch, to change her ward and give her a new bed." In response, it seemed, the demented straining women gave a chorus of groans, at various levels of agony. "Hear that, Cliff? It'll drive her round the bend, she's only twenty. I know what's going on. Get her out of here." As if reading the situation from an unbridgeable distance, Sister Annie abruptly thrust herself into the room, glancing angrily at Cliff and whispered loudly at him, "You shouldn't be in here, Mr Roberts, I told you."

"Listen, Theatre Sister Annie," said Cliff, moved for once to a sense of instant irresistible outrage, "this is my wife's first child and unless she is moved to a suitable ward, I shall consult with the doctors on duty, put in a complaint with the Registrar and sue this so-called 'Happy

House' for everything it possesses - and give the story to the local and the national press!"

Kate raised herself up again. "And if he wants a witness, I'm ready."

The confrontation had an immediate effect. Sister Annie took a step back in mild shock, such shows of spirit were rare. Yes, her prospects of promotion had been briefly challenged but she was instantly on guard, and visibly outraged – after all she had done for them! But Sister Annie was also sly as a fox. 'Think like a renard,' was her favourite motto. A devious plan was already forming in her twisted mind.

Pretending discomfiture, Sister Annie finally snapped. "Mrs Roberts was due for relocation anyway! As arranged. And please wait in the waiting area which is for visitors, I have work to do." She turned and left. Kate winked, then winced. Cliff kissed the ministering angel on the forehead, then his wife, and departed the pain-filled, little NHS black hole.

When he entered the 'waiting area', Tom, Kate's husband was there, looking out of the small dusty window at the end of the room. He was about thirty, five ten or so, brawny, with a broad face with small slit-eyes, a jutting jaw. His manner was pushy and sometimes threatening, usually for no reason. He had a broad valleys accent which was sometimes indecipherable. He faced Cliff as if they were in a boxing ring.

"Bloody well still here?" he barked, "still, nothin' we can do 'bout that!" he glanced around aggressively. "My Kate's alright, she'll pull through, I'll see to that!"

"She told me to get Mary out of there."

"Kate told me. And she's right, you'll see. Who's kiddin' who? Women are the boss. Always something there in the end for them. For her now, it's babies and she's another woman, a bleedin' mother! And what are we left with? All the nagging all over again, and a squalling brat to keep us awake all night, and keep us in order, make our lives a misery. No fun for us here. Am I right?" he paused, out of breath. "Well, what do you think?"

Cliff was thinking about the damnable infection. Wasn't it punishment enough – if it was a punishment.

"Well?"

"Sister Annie's moving Mary to another ward now."

"I told you! Bloody bitch that woman! Bloody Head Sister'? – torturer-in -Chief, more like."

The door was pushed open slowly and in entered Roy Hughes, a local man, whose wife of forty-five was having a baby."

"Well?" demanded Tom, "how is your wife?"

Mr Hughes looked alarmed, swayed and began sliding to the floor in a faint.

Tom darted forward and held him up, "It's OK, does this every time. His missus in the emergency too. He'll be around in a tick." He heaved Mr Hughes onto the grimy sofa and settled him down.

"Yes," he declared, indicating the semi-unconscious Mr Hughes "women like, have all the advantages."

For a while, they both stood staring out of the uncleaned window, wishing it was all over. Night had fallen. Cliff saw the moonlight spreading outside like some great false hope, an invitation to still gloomier speculations.

"All the advantages," repeated Tom, falling in with Cliff's darker mood.

He offered Cliff a flat bottle from his pocket. "Vodka," he said reassuringly, and took a swig. "Hell," Cliff said to himself, "why not? – 'the House of Good Cheer' is, after all, a place of joy and new life, not of frightened husbands and fearful spouses. Well, by God, like Sally, he was learning now. Tom took another swig and offered the bottle. Cliff took a couple of swallows. Both gasped in relief. They heard Mr Hughes reviving and his feet shuffling on the lino. When they turned, they saw Mr Hughes was sitting at the table working his way through the pile of tattered women's magazines, drooling over the girlie underwear ads. He seemed oblivious to everything and everybody, including his nearby wife. They supped again from the bottle.

"Kate told me to go for a drink at my local, and to take you, like, see. No point in waitin' tonight, she said, and she'll keep an eye open for Mary too."

"You've got a good un there."

"The women are in charge again. Let's go for a pint then."

A couple of hours later the pint had changed into three or four. Cliff slowed down, but Tom emptied yet another pot. "Better be off while you can still drive," he advised.

"Right then. I've got a bottle of brandy at home."

"Don't mix your drinks,' the man said."

"Usually I only drinks beer, but this is an occasion, like, right?"

Tom roughly shouldered his way through the crowd at the bar and was sober enough to find the car. After a bumpy ride, they arrived at Tom's house, a typical suburban bungalow, pebble-dashed, with bright new brittle bricks, plastic window frames, and a concrete front garden. Tom jumped out and surveyed his family palace with pride. He punched the air in salute and bawled out, "it may only be a palace but it's home!" and went inside. Tom led him into the sitting room and dived immediately for the cocktail cabinet, an imitation thirties-style polished box of chipboard, with edges splintering already. He removed a full bottle of brandy, filled two glasses to the brim, ripped off his coat, flexed his shoulders gave one glass to Cliff and raised his own. Christ, thought Cliff, got to get out of here, if it's the next thing I ever do. "Sit down, mate, we got all night." Cliff leaned back in the chair. He blinked as Tom drank two or three great gulps again

"Hey! Here's to the next generation. Let them all be boys!" he declared, trying to down the glass in one go. His eyes bulged, he sprayed the fiery liquid in all directions.

"Dammo," he protested, his throat burning, then pointing as at some invisible antagonist, "I can drink this when I want, specially whenever the old nag bag's out of the way. Bugger the women, I say every day. But my women loves this place. My Kate's golden nest. Ma-in-Law's too. Three-piece suite, wall-to-wall carpeting, cocktail cabinet, three bedrooms, garden back and front, conservatory out back, too. Ma- in-Law, her old man was a bloody dustman, called himself 'environmental engineer', never saw him except when he was trying to escape. But she knew which side her bread was buttered and who buttered it too!" He roared with laughter and gulped his drink - no spraying this time. "Bugger the women," he concluded.

"What? Even your glam Ma-in-Law?"

"You haven't seen her like she really is."

"Yes I have. Last Saturday. Afternoon visit."

Cliff remembered all right. Ma-in-Law was about fifty, overweight all over, with a spare tyre, drooping breasts and a tight mini-skirt, mascara-eyed, face painted like Cleopatra, she tottered on high heels, and had a laugh which challenged Tom's booming, rutting call. She was as coarse and mindless as he, and was proud of it. Tom was unaware of any such drawback and gloried in his dominance.

"I thought she was, well...er, quite...bubbly."

"Bag always wanted to be in the driving seat," Tom declared harshly, " – and not only 'bubbly for her age', I can tell you. But thank god, Sport on now," he reached forward, switched on the TV, slumped back in his seat, eyes glazed, and was soon hypnotized into blessed silence by the Arsenal giants versus the West Ham pygmies.

Cliff sank into the tatty uncomfortable arm chair, and quietly nodded off as the game faded, wondering again how he was going to escape.

He was awakened by a hideous yodelling sound. He rubbed his eyes and saw Tom in full pursuit galloping around the room as if hunting an animal, lashing out with an invisible whip. "Yes, you women, every fuckin' one of you!" He lashed out again at the unseen harpy, "you only want one thing, fuckin' fuckin,' and fuckin' money. Shit, in the end, they always win. We know what they're bloody well like, but then we go and fall for 'em! Fuckin' love, it's called." He dragged off his shirt, "so fuckin' hot in here. Got to piss," he declared, grabbed the bottle and lurched off to the toilet. Cliff saw that Tom was well past the sodden slow-drunk phase, he was now well into obliteration mode. Cliff had to leave. A loud crash and the sound of splintering glass came from the toilet. Hell, thought Cliff, as he rushed out to investigate – perhaps, hopefully, he'll bleed to death. The door of the bathroom was wide open, steam billowed out. Cliff heard loud splashings and gruntings. When he finally entered, he was greeted with a Tom who was now completely starkers, his remaining garments scattered soggily about. The hand-basin was full of cold water and the bidet overflowing. Tom thrust his head into both, in turn, muttering, "Hot, so fucking hot!" his body bathed in sweat and tap water. He reeled to the toilet and sat down with all his weight on the seat. It snapped like a fallen branch. Tom did not even notice the plastic fracture. He roared again, extended his arms as if he had just scored a goal and began giving sloppy military salutes to the mirror. "God bless our gracious Queen, Queen Sheila of Ponty, this is her palace. No bloody chance for us! A good fuck once..." He began to masturbate wildly and ineffectually, his member remained flaccid, the old brewer's droop, thought Cliff, about to move out. At that moment Tom leaned forward on the bidet and gave one huge retching heave. An avalanche of puke streamed out hitting his chest, thighs, and covered his crotch in thick steaming beer and lumpen brandy. Tom didn't seem to notice the stinking filth. He extended his arms again and pranced around the sodden floor, "Bloody women, no bloody chance. Kate was a grand fuck, I tell you, but look at her now! Like her Mam!" he brayed, and began masturbating again." Yes, now listen, I know her alright, why? 'cos I shagged her, yes, Kate's Mam. A one long night stand, I shagged her kneeling, I fucked her lying, if I'd had wings I'd have fucked her flying, ha, ha! Up the arse, between the tits, piggy back sucking, coming all over to her hairy slit, I did, and she came back for more. Listen now, that's God's holy truth I tell you. What d'you think?"

"Does Kate know?" Cliff finally managed, put off totally by the barking two-legged hyena in front of him.

"She shuspects something, but no more than kiss or two, see, Kate's body's just like her Mam's, yes, I shagged her all night!"

Cliff retreated to the door. Tom bent double again, gasped, and began having a hard pushing monumental shit into the bidet. It finally burst. Streaks of haemorrhoidal blood mixed with diarrhoea poured out, missed the bidet and hit the floor. Cliff felt nausea rising. He tiptoed out, carefully avoiding the broken glass of the brandy bottle. Miraculously, Tom had escaped any damage. He shut the door of the 'palace' behind him, with Tom's ravings, intemperate splashings and stool strainings still in his ears.

Outside, in the distance, he could see the horizon lightening up with a vast rosy glow. Birds began their fresh, hesitant waking chirping, then exploded into full choral majesty! What a hale, heart-warming song! Jesus, he had just spent the night with a lunatic, and was cured already! He looked around, lost at first. He had never been in this part of town before. He decided to follow the signs to the main road. There he found signposts to the hospital. He made his way up the steep streets and soon found himself outside the main door of the Maternity Unit. He saw with relief that the door was open. He made his way to the waiting room, past the receptionist's desk, empty of sweet Sally's super cosmetic smiles, empty of anyone. The infantile paper squiggles on the screens fluttered in the draught. Cliff made it to the 'waiting space' and collapsed onto the wobbly, stained sofa - enough for one day! And fell asleep.

He was awakened by the distant sounds of laughter, was it? or was it just frantic Tom braying again. He staggered blearily to his feet. The clock told him 10 am. Impossible! What was going on? Again the sounds of distant revelry. He thought of Mary. He had to find her. Had foul fiend Sister Annie moved her yet? He advanced down the corridor, the sounds of merriment getting louder. Was Mary alright? He realised he'd been incommunicado for the entire night. He paused. Yes, hell, Tom's typical brutish effusions of hollow hilarity filled the air. And yes, -it was coming from the emergency ward. He stood at the door, listening. A female voice joined in with Tom, as discordant and phony as his. Cliff felt someone push him in the back. He swung around in alarm. It was awful Theatre Sister Annie herself, her face wreathed in smiles far worse than her usual caring expression. She wore the look of a benign queen cobra about to strike. She motioned for him to go in. With a shiver of revulsion, Cliff stepped inside, anything to get out of her way. The first person he was confronted by was the outrageous Tom, but a Tom transformed. He was scrubbed and washed fresh and clean. His small eyes sparkled, clear as dew. He gave off a pleasant smell of eau de Cologne. He was wearing a yachtsman's blazer with silver buttons and a commodore hat tilted at a rakish angle. He had on patent leather shoes, and slithered around the polished floor with something like proficiency. He was performing intricate tango steps, calling time with the yowling female who Cliff now recognised was Tom's Mother-in-Law.

"Sheila, my Queen of Smiles," guffawed Tom and pointed at Cliff, "Look who's come for cocktails!"

Sheila bared her ivories, a swish model on the cat-walk now, posing for the photographers, looking down her nose at the hoi-poloi. She grabbed her partner, a willing and able Tom, and gave out one of her own ghastly, ear-busting high cheers. Tom whooped at the swoop. There was no sign of the sick beast of the night before. 'Sheila' herself was dressed to the nines she thought always suited her: black mesh tights with generous slabs of thigh bulging through, her favourite leather mini skirt, low cut blouse, with plunging decolte, frizzled hennaed hair, layers of mascara, vermilion lipstick - her scarlet woman persona. Her whole body gyrated and wobbled in pleasurable motion as she slid along the parquet. At arm's length, she tenderly held up "the most precious burden in the world," yelled Tom planting a slobbering kiss on the baby's forehead, mercifully still asleep. Sheila gave Tom a wet fleshy buss, "Best son-in-law in the land. See what he's got now! On top of our palace on the hill. And here in a flash, he knows his job," she jiggled her breasts suggestively, staring at the flabbergasted Cliff. For some reason an image of sweet Sally crossed his mind, the only one, it seemed, well out of all this, thank god!

Sheila gave Tom another smacker. "Lovely boy! My favourite Commodore of the Fleet!"

"My Queen of Smiles," Tom yodelled back and they flew into another tango routine. Still groggy from the injections, Kate stared out from her crumpled sheets. Was this some kind of joke?

"And the best Ma-in-Law in the world," Tom trumpeted, and gave the babe another kiss. Kate reached out a hand for the bundle but Sheila ignored the gesture and tangoed off.

"A baby girl," Tom carolled, making like an Argentine lover, "my favourite in the world, bibeeee girly, like Sheila here, bibeee, a great Ma, like my darlin' Kate..."

"...and Mary too," the perspiring Sheila added, nudging the silent Cliff, "Look!"

Through the swing doors entered Head Sister Annie, in victory mode. She had been busy 'inducing' both labours throughout the night in the surgery ward, without mishap, so that the two new Mams would soon be on their way out of her life and her ascent to the skies. Exit! Simples. Sister Annie was wheeling a steel-framed hospital bed, bright with fresh linen and a new patient stirring in it – Mary. She was dazed but triumphant, drained but recovering, the stain of the infection expunged. On her breast rested a baby girl, as quiet as Kate's. Thank god, noted Cliff, the god of silence is on the men's side this time! Head Sister Annie parked the comatose Mary next to Kate and retreated to the door, a Nightingale triumphant.

"Another girl on top of it all," yowled Tom. "What luck we mere men have at the end, four lovely ladies, four gorgeous Mams, and Head Sister Annie to conduct it all," he whipped off his cap and saluted her smartly three or four times, "Commodore Thomas reporting Ma'm, four happy girls each with a silver lining!"

Theatre Sister Annie nodded to the spluttering, sliding loon and retreated to the door. Tom plunged his hand into his bag under the bed and came up with a bottle of champagne. He flourished it like a club. Everyone cheered - though Cliff's 'hooray' was somewhat muted. Head Theatre Sister Annie Smith surveyed the merry gang, beaming hideously over their undoubted joy. "Now this is how it is, they'll see," she thought and gave them one last unforgettable smile and closed the door, "The House of Good Cheer" she murmured in farewell," that's what this is really all about, isn't it?!"

Home Thoughts

"Dylan Thomas Centenary Celebrations in Overdrive!" Western Mail Feb 7th 2014

After forty years, I stood on the Bristol suspension bridge again, rudely staring at my nation, Wales, and was suddenly dumbstruck. For the first time I realised Wales was not just one enormous cow-pat, but consisted of thousands of the little platters, spreading out in all directions, each its own shitty little principality, each possessing its own fortified White Tower - the Town Hall - its own Council-Tax Laundry Department, (robbing the poor to pay the rich), its own Green Hell Makers, Weights and Measures Saboteurs, Pot Hole Planners, Small Print Purveyors, its own mob of soft-brained Aldermen-Yes-Men, full of dress uniforms, always with a royal to lick up to, short fat Mayors, at this moment in time, all backed up by the smashing local Constabulary Marauders, strike breakers to a man! Bless our brave HQ's local heroes, I say, in spite of suffering from ever-present outbreaks of sleeping sickness in all ranks – Croeso Cymru, in the end, a land of near total whisky-amnesia, the whole spreading brownfields giving the world a false impression of the oneness of Wales and the wholesomness of Welsh respectability - as, yes, it had so deceived me for so long! - whereas there was nothing much there at all, except the big-deal thespians, man - the sham hams - the girl sopranos with their ridiculous homunculuses , the insane sheep, dyed-in-the-wool hypocrites, the general tribal myopia and, of course, the entirely satisfactory amounts of drinking and fornicating - not in bits and pieces either, heavy, man! - stuff like that! Why, every Sunday morning the turf itself heaves in every Chapel graveyard as even the dead join in the merry sex-making - O bless those immortal crevices of delight! In a flash, I could perceive all that now, a Damascene vision from the valuable economic asset of a bridge. I was on the road to majestic Splott in Cardiff - now no kidding, man, no hoax in sight, I had been invited by the organs of parochial righteousness to visit the new centres of excellence which the old imperial satrapies and protectorates of Taffswazia offered the well-oiled anglefied traveller, not such as me, for I am Tom Tell Truth, the old Demetian himself, but they knew not the monuments of the Dylan Marlais Thomases, the scattered Sons of the Wave over the land of my ancestors, the pale lurkers of poesy, were here or there. So I said to the mask in disguise from the Order of Deep Nodders in the Department of Pointless Commotion, "I'll come and have a look, then," and I went and here am I!

As I skidded to a halt outside Splott's electrifying emporium, the worthies of Wales, lined up on the marble itself, gave one mighty fart to speed me on my way. What the hell, wrong address! - they'd tried to frame me already, put me off their foul scent, the worms in the Welsh canker, but I was determined never to be scooped up like a lump of icy vanilla from a cart! They'd learn! They'd soon find out! I realised at once that it was Swansea I was supposed to be going to, see, where all the sweaty lucubrations was, laced with the top magic of the Mabinogion, and all the stunning creative crescendoes of Gwalia, all packaged for overseas trade, a penny for a three-pack - Dylan Drops, Elixers of Marlais the Tommoscine Mushrooms, if you please, variously named as you can pretty well tell, in the faggots and cheese Market, next to Salubrious Passage where all the brilliant Taff shitterati still hang out. (What a lot is packed into those few words there!) A tall Officer of the Extemporaneous Drama Volunteers awaited me - a man blessed with various ranks and titles, Commissar Curator, Able Intern, Cast Eradicator, all first class, of course, to go with the glittering stars, sashes and orders on his mighty breast, a frequent sight in those nauseous dens of cow-patted veniality - golden pensions blessing every one. And why not? Was he not a fine-grained person, of very few knots, a worthy representative of the old Welsh Arts Cloaca, an ancient body well known for its kindly, light-hearted outlook on Man and Mankind. Why my Co-convener Co-conceptualist, that was his moniker formal-like, could swear one-thousand miles an hour without attracting the odium of the podium, his charm was that strong. But what did it for him was the fact that he was also Tyrant of the Ten Thousand Sycophants of Splott, the Crowned King-Emperor of Welsh Wallets, First Secretary Manipulator of Public Pelf and, low blow here - Official Sultan of Sarcasm in the Halls of Eastern Ease – little wonder there was so much power in his head!

A cab belched past. I glanced in astonishment, for on its doors were writ the words, “Do not go gentle...” and on Tacsi number 15 behind, late as usual, “Rage, rage against the...” then three brazen tourist charabancs, with their deadly blind spots at the ready, scrawled to bits; pale white delivery vans with a lot to say but nothing to deliver; fire-engines with their obedient tenders, every inch of each winch scripted like hell! What biro-tyro had come up with all this Parnassian flim-flam? Bless you, Dylan, through it all, you patriot of Llareggub, you Lord of Libation, you Messiah of the Enlarged Pentameter, you remained tipsy to a man! I noted there were banners in the wind at every egress with the name DT signed on them in huge ink. Oh, what rich hollows within, I thought, what egregious place- names without! TV screens were lit up higher up, like in Times Square, USA, showing *Under Milk Pudding* with Elizabeth Taylor in, all the time. There were discarded brochures fluttering about too, trod-on- poesy for the masses at every step. The Llareggub verses recited by the Rev Ely Jenkins were stamped on pennants which streamed in the firmament, all over the how-green-was-my valley of night-soil Wales, in every crook and nanny. Then, damn me, a flyer flew up and flapped me in the face. I read it out, “No-Welsh-writer-can-earn-his-bread-in-Wales-unless-he-pulls-the-forelock.-Wales-is -the Land-of-my-Fathers’ –and-they-can-keep-it!” I waggled the message to my Guide. He exploded, “Haven’t had one of those for years. Ignore it. Some damnable rotter. Never D T’s! Take no notice, it is an unforgivable swindle and all wrong. Dung on it!”

He chucked it back into the treacherous eddies with a flick of an elegant wrist. Meanwhile, whichever way I looked I was positively drowning in the super delirious Dylanomania I was dying for. My brillcreamed Mentor suddenly bellowed at me as we swept up glittering Cwmdonkin Drive, "Wales has changed! Look around, look you. Have you ever seen so many stale Welsh-cake souvenir delicatessens, or second hand condom machines, traditional Tampax boutiques, genitalia done in slate for sale on the pavement, and daffodil quims fluttering in the breeze, we have now proclaimed it all over Silurian territory itself - Mam-Wales is a sex-machine cum Drama Panorama of one thousand and one years of age, more than it took for even Helen to launch just one of her perfect faces! Bitch! Look!" The man pointed, "Gaze on my civil slaves from HQ struggling to get in, the turnstiles bobbing up and down, they are the only ones who can afford the prices, even with buckets–full of lickspittle thrown in."

The Fab Facilitator shone with pride, smoothed down his head, waved his arms in conviction mode, his eyes a steely glow, as in the grip of sheer masturbation.

"We have purchased up the entire approaches and Hall of Residence of early Dylan," he went on, grinding his teeth and pounding his palm, "and converted it into a permanent exhibition pavilion and promenade of Dylan's boyhood muse of paradise, Xana-dewi. People, sing your heart out!" He threw another switch which revealed a vista of Dylan at Collonus, Bangor, the World - an old man with bloody eyes, a classic tragedy of antique Llanelly! Such is it!

Now to the piece of resistance! My crafty Dominator reversed two levers, and I saw at once it uncovered the subtle conker heights of the new Imperium of Wales. He gripped me forcefully by the finger, and enunciated, "here are my Vestibules of Tremendousness, each apse, alcove, nave, colonnade, gazebo, billiard saloon and slave quarter owe their very existence to little old magnificent me! These are the external manifestations of the great I am; inside, my teeming brain-box boils and bubbles, the very heart and semen of my own personalised transparent cavern in there, the Mother of all Vestibules, man, eco me!" How he swelled up, how his bare chest quivered as he took out his Main Man baton and waved it at the ewe-eyed sheep in the voters' booths of Gwent. How far above all was he, how muscular yet delicate was his very stance! "And don't you ever forget it," he thundered to a close, overcome by saliva and slyness. "Yes," he asseverated on, "each worm-hole is a permanent sort of grave-rave, and all due to Wales the Brave, namely, me again! Like I said, didn't I? Yippie-aye a!"

I did not venture to contradict him as he introduced me to anther vast ante-chamber of Tremendousness, "bigger than the Reichstag one of mighty German Adolf!" he carolled, " Zeig heil! Ich bin my own do-it-yourself apotheosis, and do not you ever forget that either!" He grunted as he switched on the two-hundred or so huge swasticoed chandeliers. I stepped back in awe and gasped at what I saw. Ranged ahead of me stood what looked like a whole reserve series of new expansive Mexican cave entrances, fresh, well placed, full and rounded as hell, with the sound of captive Aztec humming-birds rising from gilded cages somewhere in the distance.

"Makes the hell-hole of the Boulevard Hall of the British Museum look like a bird box!" he trilled. "What a sight and sound for the old language of our drooling Taffo-thicko OAP's!" he snapped out, revealing his contempt for the ordinary man in Queens Gate Mews, and me as well. I had just celebrated my eighty-second birthday. First rate snake in the ass!

So this spread was it! I was at last confronted by the immense authentic quality of Wales's one thousand and one cultivated Arts Empires, for those curving thresholds were picked out in slab Victorian brown, the colour of the Great Stink, but then I saw the speckled brownages were spread out in delicious little mini-dollops like the larger picture; the whole site seemed that of an exploded mammoth, a vista of whirring brown fragments and turdy oscillations in every direction, from bored hole to bored hole, all with the unmistakable stamp of Wales, the puce dragon on a yellow background with untrimmed nails, belching out fake flames held aloft by the over bare-ing Saint Trinian blouses of Splott, with the elusive Prime of Primes, the arch-creator Dylan hisself, supping a quart at the Mythical Beast Pub in the posh Uplands of Swansea where the likes of him and me do dwell..."

"...I should think so - I don't think!" he muttered out loud, a pathetic sarcasm, now in the public domain, condemning him forever!

"Those rugby barrels of theirs up there, are always near-by," I uttered instead, "they have 'dear is my country to me' inscribed all over them!"

"One of my best lines," my frothing Literary Installator burbled out and motioned me onwards on this quite devastating tour of Greater Taffia, probing into each mind-blowing catacomb for his Sultan's sake – he felt so important, I could see that, and that was vital! - him chattering like a rat trying fuck a bat the while, while I bent my arm at his knee, clever boots me, O rara avis, I had convinced them all. The duped leader just prattled on and on like an old baby's rattle. The agent provocateur in me urged him on, "as for the disfrenchified voters of Wales and their awareness as just how awful they are, you might as well play a bassoon to an earthworm!" "Bravo!" he brayed and caloo-callayed for a while, then changed the subject to one closer to his ghastly heart - but then remained mute as a mirror. Well, I had to say something, so I said, "Well, you don't say."

"That's because I am yours truly tremendous!" he was tight-lipped back. "Look you on!" he urged and he switched on the automatic Dylan recording in all the accents of the world. The miraculous line was, peculiarly enough, "Do not go gentle into that good night...' first in a Welsh accent, then American, southern style, then Pawnee, Inouit, Patagonian, Galician, Breton, Mann and Jersey, same words, different music, each line a masterpiece. Then, my bouncy SS runic Leader suddenly shrieked and jumped backwards, staring out loud, for the voice had got out of control. These were its very words, a funny spoken at speed non-stop: "Now to DT's favourite-joke!-he-was-in-a-big palace-down-in-the-cellars - trap doors-in-the-floors - he lifts-one-up-and-looks – down-there-a-cellar-full-of-liquid- heifer-diarrhea - with-all-the-worthies-of-Wales, up-to-their-lips–in- it, singing-in-one-breathless-chorus-their-new-national-anthem, "Please don't make a wave! Please don't make a wave!"

My Mentor stood lips aghast, hands shielding his shocking face, "What a repugnant even thought!" He gagged, stacatto-like, "some malefactor from over the border, not DT's favourite joke. The opposite, it was Dylan's most hated funny, I knew him well, don't take any notice, you have a whole lifetime of servility ahead of you. Let's hit the road, man!"

We strolled over to the waiting stages. More gigantic Gothic letterings hung over each germ-free enter sign, notices of an inspirational kind, but softened by less threatening invocations like 'Arbeit Macht Frei,' and above the old Arts Cloaca Hole, 'abandon hope all ye who defecate here - ' to which my Interlocutor gave the distinguished outstretched caesarean salute "Cor, shag a bag, those was the days!" he gushed at his own nostalgia and penetrated the shadows. A sheet of A4 wrapped round his nose, he read it bellowing indignantly, "Palaces-and-mansions, like-stables-and-sties, can-still-be – the-haunt, of-asses-and-flies!" – Imbloodypossible!" he gnashed his teeth like a polar bear and shredded the blasphemy with his grimy paws. He finally ignored it and passed inside to the next concavity.

I made out at once out a hundred sample cases with toys of lead, decked out in gorgeous pretend-costumes just like my Guide-Deviser's as a Druid. They stood proudly outside replicas of the most decent places of Wales to stay at, like the spot over which the Welsh Arts Cloaca had once squatted, the agate corridors of the Underdone

Assembly, the Poets' Teen Latrines, and the sweeping banisters of the Theologium Collegium of Lampeterium where so many of us learned to wank and pray. I noted with awe how my Marvellous Mentor juggled these outstanding figures about, so he could be top gun of every historic champion as he was so moved. Being Honorary Colonel of the Cenotaph Regiment of the Dead was not enough and he promoted himself up as Otto von Valhalla, Boss of all SS Volk, Reichtag, Germania, the World. Then he gave one little leap of sphincter-like pleasure, and plunged into a short blunt black corridor leading to the inner lecture halls of the Royal Society of Royal Societies. He was there, ape-like Speaker now of the disorderly Arse of Commons, propelling me yet upwards until we rounded a nicotined corner and confronted, for me, a definite odd sight - in the demi-darkness sat a hunched–up figure on a rush-bottomed chair, and that figure was clinging to the belching bubbling boiler of the central heating system, keeping his tootsies warm and his writing finger full of throbbing hot Welsh monometer expletives, just like that, and, I tell you, that braveheart of a bard was scribbling like mad on a school exercise book lots of highly great and original poems, 'Do not go... rage, rage... in my craft,' they were all there already, I could see over his shoulder. "There," commented the Leader, in very undertones, "is here, where Dylan wrote his verse in deep midwinter. He never fell off that chair. And the waste-paper basket was never wasted, such was the fairy fluency of his cerebellums. Now, we have this whole scene in replica alabaster, the Boiler Poet Scene, it's called, it's proving a great little seller too, the humbleness of him appeals to all benighted humanity outside us, I'd say. I'll get a set for you, half price, don't you worry. But there are other choice choices too. Look, the Dylan in posture series, Dylan puking, retching, honking, flicking ink, jerkin', burpin, spluttering, peeing into the sands of time, all hand-painted ; here, eating jelly-babies while reading school-boy detective yarns; more Dylan pix here, saluting me, signing my books for me, a rare distinction there, and look, old Mr President Carter's changed the US flag for Dylan, to - 'E pluribus, ME!", the 'me' being 'me' of course. Voila then, a mere selection of the Beatitudues of Wales in the Dylanosphere, a showcase for the outer reaches of the cosmos!" He paused. "I have prepared this box for you." He gave me it officially, and in it went into my back-pack quite openly and I read it out, "Dylan-is-shaving-now, lather-on-his-chin, the-razor-rasping, the-furious-strokes, the-eyes-bathed-in-alcohol; the-flushed-cheeks-soaked-in-beer, the-guttural muttering, the-wet-head-full-of-horrors, his-mirror-reflects-yet-cannot-hold-the-frightful apparition-of-a-mortal-brother..."

"Never go on"! he yelled turbulently.

"...that's Jaques Chessex!" I broke out," I'd recognise him a mile upwind among the vines."

"Disgusting outburst whatever the cost!" said my now unsentimental Firing Squad Addict, "toss that Swiss garbage aside in a heap."

"But he won the Prix Goncourt with it once upon a time!" I stood up for my principles, however brave, "the first non-Frenchman ever to win that cordon bleu trophy."

"Fackin bit of froggy tinsel! Fackin' tripehound!" he belched voluminously, "god help the triple agent when I catch up with him. But now come and see some proper fame!" He darted down a side-tunnel, marked "Fans!" Before me again up-rose the whole of St Trinian's girl Prefects, guys, swelling out like soiled blouses on a line - all under the jaundiced eyes of phosphorescent skies, I may add! So romantic!"

"God!" he simply shouted out of the blue, and plucked up a figurine and picked it, "Pig snot and cats piss, what is this again? Regard the bloody thing - a blasted Congo adulterated vegetarian pigmy, I do declare, with apple-eating cannibals of the East Indies, rotten to the core! With bits of fruity-tutti stuck on! Revolting! Off! Off! What presumption! How did they sneak in?"

“Never mind, “ I riposted more verbiage to dispel his questioning glance – “fleshpots galore in these glaring ducal ponds, swan songs for pens, evaporation for ink, home of the disappeared I’d say. Hey, look at the Ayahtola Bin Dylans there waving their most recent trimeters, not a single Koran in sight! See, the entire population *of Under Milk Pudding*, in bloody gilt, gold lame, in…” he cut right across my penetrating consonants.

“*Our* personal uniforms!” he hissed, intensely outraged, “ours to wear out. How did they get them on in here. I’m pulling them all off, I’m putting them out beyond the Pale!” He rejected them in piles. “Hell, where from did they come? Nothing to do with you, is it!?”

“Never in a Satan of sinful Sundays!” I protested like a vampire teenager in heat.

“Fine, then! They belong only to the Cellar of Duff Mementoes!” He hurled the final offending items to the ground, and quite rightly too, pissed all over them.

“Now back to the brown purlieus of Dylan,” he chimed in, and with one fell sweep across a map, pinned down the endless artistic dust-bowls of Wales in choice periods, “parishes and hundreds, Marcher Lords and Bastards, one thousand Chieftains of the Peak, so to speak, twenty two nation states, 69 Presidential Candidates, all singing like chains in the sea, …” he smirked like a politician, satisfied with his marvellous quote - yes, he knew he was as humorous as the stars above. “A moveable feast day for me ,” he commented indicating some of Dylan’s global fanatics on the screen, “note the Apache Recitation Warriors, the Zulu Impi Soneteers, with their yodelling lady-girl male matrons, the Blackfoot Spearwomen, the Maori Majorettes, swinging sexameters to a man, the entire Pawnee nation, experts in the dreaded trochee, all descendents of Geronimo, who could spot a mixed metaphor from the face of an Alpine glacier - Mr Humphries there, who took over from the great Capone, Chicago branch, specialist, in private of course, of the bra-wearing CIA Directors of the St David's day Massacre! How they all lay down their arms, and legs, for Dylan! This here was after Dylan's last Lecher Tour, long before he had those final 987 whiskies - I'm talking bottles, of course." Then I put in, I had to say something round about Dylan on his Thirtieth Birthday to the outer moons of Jupiter, else I was done for, "Creator of supernova orders of odes!" I proclaimed, "which rise out the crotch of perspiration over down by up there, the domestic boiler stance! And listen," I perorated, "buddy boy, those who came to scoff, remained to drink!" I ejaculated out with it at the end. My Gilded Praetorian, now heaped up with his chains of office, roared his approval and dragged me out, passing, as we went, a young boy reading classics. He chanted as we passed, "Peace-will-be-and-soul be free, Who February's stone takes up, Wise is he and serene will be, Who drinks for an Amethyst Cup!"

"The amethyst is a prophylactic against drunkenness," I hastened to add.

"Twice as loathsome!"" shot out my Censor, and flattened the academic lad with a top upper cut, "shit in a bin, it is no sin to have a taste for gin! Bollocks to the lot of them!" and he barrelled us into another green and pleasant cavern, boasting Wales's chief architectural delights, a panorama of pebble-dash abortions, the very House on a Breakback of Rocks, the spine-tingling Writing Shed, the exquisite shape of the perfectly formed Boat House, with the dilapidated, owl-haunted, ivy-covered Castle Towers close by, where lived the all-Welsh novelist Richard Hughes - actually something true, at last. My Guide pointed at the chicken-coop, ticky-tacky torture-chambers, "see there, well, the Leader of the Opposition has sworn that by the end of this century every family will have a Shed of Excellence like that, in every front parlour, and those of higher civic rank like me, a boat house replica, however far from the sea it may be, and for high-flyers like me again, an entire Cwmdonkin Drive blown up out of all proportion so I can piss on it after a big binge, and a second mini one, done down, so it can fit into my toilet as I praise the great constructivist, Dylan, the Vitruvius of the block, with my trousers down about my balls and cock!"

"What was your prior name?" I asked the seedy, vulgar creep.

"Dame Armitage Shanks," he moued shyly, a beacon in all that gloom. "You'll find me every night at the Bible and Black Manhattan Cocktail Bar near the giant capstan."

"And the dread thing," I hurried on becoming more aware as I went on, "is that sets of these toys are the veritable mental core of the admirable Parochialees, and Mediocraties – and the 'crachach', the crach, or scabs, as our leaders are known in the English tongue, the bosses, the leading shafts of darkness of our government, forever clothed in their silver dungarees, castrator scissors always in hand..."

He was turning white with my transpirations, when I interjected in to stop him short, "hey, look at that flashing metaphor on the heights!" Look, above Liz Taylor. I spelled the words coming out, "I-am-a-Welshman-who-does-not live-in-his-own-country-because- I -still-want-to eat-and- drink!"

"That's not DT's again! Perish the thought!" my Sultan of Sarcasm growled and waved his index finger, indicating the more heroic replicas of DT's, "these are the real Dylans!" He cursed the lying lumiere up there again, "that most notorious trick-blinking is not for true believers right here in Splott," he yelped, "whoever is doing this to me is a dead hunted duck, I promise all our more bigoted clients. Tight-arsed. You'll see! But onwards now to something healthier and much more normal, our Awardees Awards. He rapidly condemned out of hand the furtive postal services and the nasty telegrams, "hey, you up there, you don't put me off with your dirty diatribes, you messengers from the dead, no escapegoats in my old pals act! Hey, Twm or Tom, you gotta move on! You see the Ambulatory gift packs here, brown envelopes crammed with crinkly greens, random as hell, especially for the last late artists.

This is how the protocol works - Gareth, Dai, Luned, here passing by haplessly, see, are given 500 pounds in broad daylight, like that, like that, like that, simple hand outs, no receipts anywhere, just first names will do for Accounts, your wallets can rest easy - all awardees must be anonymous to keep it fair and free, - and tickets for the white-suited first night penguins, over down by the Opera pissoires. But how to control any buggering toy nay-sayers, those disgusting slips of the tongue, wretched denizens of used toilet paper, how!? Lo, see, over down by up there, my Berserker Grenadiers on the Barrack Square, down there my shocking troops on their flanks, the fearsome Ossificator Animators, one burp from you during the main aria means one touch of their deadly pacific wands, and you instantly become stone, mere stone, like in the ground, muddied, defuncted, deaded, goned. Plus our brave Lank Skirmisher Probers, our Ten Logistic Commandments over there, with their mortal Animators and Obfuscatorial Squads, to keep the climate calm, the cuckooes in their nests, the radicals down the plughole, and the Tremendous, US, always ahead. Yes, innovative events are never 'Everests' for me. Why, just one poem of my lot modified the frontiers of Albania forever - that was due mainly to the one thousandth and one Spenserian Stanza, never to be trifled with. But behind the pomp and power, Opera nose-dived, for example, but my recently impressed Rock Re-animators moved in and the rot moved out, bloody vagabond-vanguards, the long-haired, tennis-shoe pervert wearers, down with their obscene 'e' mails– I have the potency to reduce them to the condition of reddish terracotta twerps! And I would remind you," there was no blocking his muddy stream, "that it is humiliating for a man of my standing to put a mouse on trial for manslaughter..."

"...no, it is not!" I finished for him. He stood, his whole body agape, ears cocked for the faint voices, tenor and bass, floating over the surges of the sea. "Please don't make a ..."

"...never! Cut that out forever!" he went on bended knee and covered his ears. "That's not just an order, it's do or die!"

The anthem hovered a moment or two in the air like a sick helicopter. My Mentor sprang about, giving ordures to down below.

"Throw in the Ossificators en masse!" my still grotty batty eminence grise trumpeted, and in a second the lead figurines froze even more solidly and went still.

"There they go, the stiffs," he carolled, " they will be dispatched to the Carousel of Agony at dawn and tortured back to life in the hideous Memory of Nightmare Arcades, the tomb of the Liberties of Wales!"

God, he looked so bloody in the limelight, I have to say, but he seemed to be drawing to some kind of conclusion. Overall, in spite of bureaucratic excesses and blotting paper landslides, I was happy to be a witness to so many familiar strange phenomena - the awesome profile of the lava-bread of Wales, for example, still more elevated, still more bronzed, and so much more tomorrow, and all bear the hue of dew on a bog in smog on her face, Mam-Cymru's to a 't', – bravo Mammo!" Well, in spite of snipings, metal and mental, expulsions and poison gas attempts, it was nice to know I'd had a glimpse of the true Taffucks of life, however worrisome. 'Twas the overall tremendousnesses of it wot done it - the Mexican cave entrances, the inky yellowing banners, the greyish rigid figurines set in concrete, the handsome brown envelopes, the silly jejune Gueveras, the rancid home-grown voters cast aside, the smart post-cards of Offa's Dyke, the Hadrian's Wall of Wales, keeping all other opinions out forever. But I saw him peering around, smelling out the turncoat deadly-nightshade Trotsky-Quisling. Who was it really who had fucked up the malodorous jamboree of the glorious, multifarious Dylan centenary Celebrations announced in The Western Mail? I saw the question writ across his veined orbs. We now stood in mutual suspicious valedictory suspense on the suspension bridge. I pointed out the howgreens of my nation over there and admitted my guilt, open as a Venus fly-trap for a dunce to drop into! It did. His face was immediately wreathed with viciousness and he glared at me with his expression, "so you are the two-faced flapping labial back-slider, the crimson stab in the back as well - the Indian in the woodpile!?" he asserted agressively, aside on every side, "Twm the toilet tissue traitor all along! I told them in Cardiff to fart you in the opposite direction, just in case, but they would not listen. And you have been opening my postscripts, I can tell by your quotations, I have I hit the nipple on the ripple, am I right?" He pointed with sharpened eyes and yelled over the sand-bars far below, "Aux Armes, Aux Armes, mes braves, on parade, full battle order, my Obscurantists, Obfuscators, Berserkers, Nitpickers, Ossicators and tall-in-the-saddle security skirmishers, gold pilferers, false prophets, hangers on, scrap iron hunters, marvellous mayoralties, all tremendous sods of the capital's Splott machine, now, I urge you like mad, all unite under the banner of the Ales of Wales, in the White Towers, never to allow another alien miscreant-emigrate like this peasant penny-whistle-blower Twm the Useless, herein or in here."

"Yes," I sang out, back, "the people of Wales will one day definitely comprehend all the brown droppings of Splott Hall, their rich greed blazoned on every bank statement, and all its foregoing, it will out! So for now, my Guardian Pimp of all Ordures, my belle Dame Armitage Shanks, Queen of the U Bends, in your typical ghastly Poet Centenary Year, hail and fuck off!"

He turned puce and marched off, shuffling nevertheless. His dim words echoed across the usual Channel, dead as toe-nail parings. His day was done OK, but not his new anthem and the coming waves! And the land of my Fathers was still over by there, just like me! Staring hard again at Wales, the final vision came to me:

'My dream is done, my agony spent,

Old Tom Tell Truth for you was meant,

So take Twm's part, truth has no end,

And learn the ways of the heart.'

A Poet is...

...Lord of the Horizon,

Sun Grazer,

High Fiver, Cloud Rider,

Objective correlater,

Sugar-lipped literalist of the Imagination,

Unacknowledged legislator of the world –

Brushed off, like lichen from a rock.

The Archivist and his Man

The Archivist stood in his cellar before the old banks of ancient office files. They were made of solid oak with a brass frame on the front for the identification cards. Now they were all going to be digitalised and the technicians needed to know which subject they were dealing with – 'building regs,' 'comm tax,' 'education,' 'environment ,'etc. The Archivist had ordered the cards to fit the slots. Today it was 'education' for the changeover. The Archivist's assistant, Emlyn Hughes, bald, fifty, shakey, anxious, always out to do his best, however badly, entered carrying a cardboard box.

"Ah," said the Archivist, "that was quick, Emlyn."

"Though I hurried, "remarked Elfin respectfully, "I been that careful with this lot, sir." Emlyn was immensely willing, which made him popular, however mistaken he might be. The Archivist had noted that Emlyn had no qualifications for working in archives, but he was at his last gasp and this was his final job at the Town Hall. His only universally acknowledged qualification was that he had been married five times, was currently going though his latest annulment and was a rich source of divorce law for his colleagues. He would shake to breaking point as he confided the details of his most recent marital disasters to his colleagues, but no one seemed to mind and listened to him to the end, regardless of his moist handkerchief as he mopped his brow.

Emlyn loved 'his' Archivist , "you can say anything to him and he never minds. No judgements. A real gentleman!" The Archivist had given him the chore that morning of preparing the education cards for the wooden cabinets, and, lo! - he had them ready, already! Emlyn picked up a few cards and passed them to his benign Master.

"Very neat," said the Archivist approvingly. The Card E-D-UC, he spelled it out - 'educ' he added, pronouncing the letters as one word. He fitted the card into its brass frame. "Perfect ,' he said. Perhaps there was room in the office for Emlyn after all, he reflected as he moved along the cabinets, fitting the cards into their slots. He took up another card and began to fit it in. He came to an abrupt halt. He examined the next few cards in the box, held one up and shook it quizzically at Emyr .

"Yes, sir, very 'neat' this time, sir, as you say."

"E-D-U-C, the Archivist spelled it out, 'Educ,' here" said the Archivist, "is right, but..." he held up the next card, "look, E-D-C-U – 'edcu' is not right."

"EDCU is not right..." Emlyn echoed, his voice trailing away.

"E-D-U-C, 'educ', is right."

"E-D-U-C, 'educ ' is right," Emlyn whispered.

"E-D-C-U, 'edcu,' is not.

Emlyn blanched, his hands began to wobble. Not again. His new job was flitting away already.

"Never mind... " said the Archivist kindly - he would keep on Emlyn – a real treasure after all!

"...we all make mistakes, but just one thing, Emlyn, please – something you alone know in all the spacious civic offices of the world, can you explain to me, how, just how can a man get to be so wrong?"

The Day of the Quail

People said it was an odd day, but for Bryn Jones it was quite normal. He was walking down the High Street of the dilapidated, emptied, ghost settlement of Pentre Ifan in the glorious far West of rural Wales, Bryn's home town, a place visitors avoided on sight. The countryside however was still inhabited, but mainly by employees of the vast National Park, fugitive academics searching for Arthur's Seat amid the crags and caves above the waves down the coast, elusive native hill farmers with their tasty sheep, and crowds of back-packing hikers and trekkers out for an elevated environmental thrill.

Bryn reached the run-down market square, the decayed heart of the dying town. The square was infested by hords of bats in the belfry of the boarded up church, which no Pest Controller seemed to notice or care much about. Next door stood an old Victorian library building with a prominent notice on the front door announcing its closure and imminent destruction. Its replacement was to be a squat Tesco store, limited by space but perfect fodder for shrinking Pentre Ifan. The old grammar school-house opposite was now used as an occasional hall for the Women's Institute and Boy Scout meetings. The few shop front windows were strewn with empty files, discarded free newspapers, uncollected mail and broken office equipment. The shops which were still open were laid out with sorry displays of second-hand goods, cheap chipped pottery, cracked glassware, garments donated from the dead and buried, smelling of washing powder and decomposition. The goods seemed to go in circles, from the needy to the needless, all on a summer's day. Business was sluggish as usual.

Bryn said a prayer as he passed the stripped, rejected library. He looked with distaste at the sole pub, the Rising Sun - more like 'setting,' Bryn muttered to himself. It dispensed stale beer, at inflated prices, when open. Its woodwork was unpainted and peeling, old mottled brown Victorian tiles glistened on the outside walls. Close by was a nescaffé caff, with creaking chairs, stained table tops, unswept floors, the local refuge of the burgeoning body of myriad pauper oldies. Around every entrance of these sad emporiums, open or closed, were chocolate wrappers and ripped newssheets whirling in the wind. The few stalls in the open area in front were laid out with plastic bric-a-brac 'bargains,' tinny kitchen utensils all the way from Tashkent, one-pound children's book-gifts also found in the cancer and heart attack shops. The stall-holders, mostly sat vacant-eyed on their wobbly, camping stools, rubbing their empty, mittened hands from time to time, reaching for the ever present comforting cup o'char close by. Other sellers sounded maniacally cheerful as they yelled out the virtues of their bedraggled cabbages and carrots and the supremacy of their mattresses and mesh curtains.

To the sense of helplessness of both shoppers and stall-holders, was added the seemingly universal physical deformity of obesity. In all his travels Bryn had never seen such waves of lapping fat, bulging bellies, massively drooping buttocks, of both men and women. Their ballooning clothes, he noted, were either straight out of the charity shops or going straight in to them. Their shopping baskets were never full of food, but packed with boxes of dinky donuts, cream slices, chicken nuggets , crisps - 'caviar to the general' !

Bryn looked around for greengrocer Ben, everybody's favourite. There he was, sitting among his pomegranites, setting out his Spanish grapes and English strawberries. Tall lean, bald and a grandfather, he was invariably cheerful, one of God's genuine genial souls. "How's it going?" asked Bryn. "Great," said Ben with enthusiasm, "they can't get enough of my pomegranites!".

"And your kids? "

"One boy's just passed his A's, the other got accepted at College, and my girl's going into nursing. All decided this morning, so it's good day to you." He doffed his peaked cap, and laughed. It was a totally genuine sound of pure joy, one hundred per cent, and reflected his celebration of the ups and downs of life, come what may. But Bryn knew Ben's old Mam had just died in hospital, of lack of nutrition it was said; one son had just been charged with drug possession, the other with GBH, and the girl transported to hospital, with her new baby, after a suspected overdose. Bryn knew too, as everyone at the market did, that Ben was on the brink of bankruptcy and had spent the last two weeks in a tent in the woods with his sons. Today he was finally emerging. He confided to Bryn that he had now found a marvellous old period cottage in the Vale for his deserving, supportive family. Bryn bought half a dozen pomegranites, laughed along with Ben at the dolorous pedestrians who looked sick and tired of just about everything, but, they both noted, some of them wore happy expressions, "like grins on huge boiled eggs" Ben remarked, but in a very sympathetic manner. Bryn moved on with a goodbye wave, feeling better, as everyone did, after a chat with the beaming Ben. If only, he thought, the large ones of the world could laugh at their own condition like the grand old greengrocer.

Bryn bought the gardening gloves he was after and stuffed them into his pocket. The flower displays were already wilting in the dried-out display buckets. The owners would be abandoning them at the end of the day. Most of the folk knew there was little future here, a grimy fading patch on the poisonous trail left by burned-out coal tips and exhausted mines, peopled by queer and fading ghosts. The sole compensation, Bryn thought, was that the entire population seemed to be quietly going nuts, quite amiably, a condition Bryn thought both fitting and worthy of mirth. He luxuriated in these states of mild moon-madness whenever he encountered them, indeed occasionally making his own original contributions.

Bryn glanced at the library, then came to an abrupt halt. An affectionate smile spread over his face. Emerging from the doors was his father, 'the Dad', the most respected man in town, retired school head teacher, local historian and scholar. He refused to move away from the place, the area where his forbears had lived and which was full of the beloved histories he always wrote up as short stories. The family lived on the outskirts of town in Hendre, 'Home,' and it was. Bryn was taking his annual holiday from teaching.

"Hi, Dad!" he called out. 'The Dad' paused and looked his son up and down as if for the first time. "Boy," he finally said, "there is only one thing wrong with you, your legs are too short for your body."

Bryn looked down at his stunted extremities. "Well, well," he said. "I think you're right again. More books?" He gestured at the plastic shopping bag the Dad was carrying.

His father nodded, "there is no end to families in all genealogies," he said, "especially ours."

"There's an end to libraries, Dad."

"But not of books." He raised the bag.

"Then let's get a nescaffé. "

"You buy, but I won't drink," said the Dad.

"OK, then. Come on."

He ushered the Dad into the darkened hole, smelling of yesterday's re-used Brazilian grains, the counter tended by a girl scarcely out of single-figure age, but she was cheerful among the slops. Dad settled down in a rickety chair. "Your Mam wants you to stay longer," he said.

"Thanks Dad, I was just thinking of that. I'll give the College a ring. It'll be OK."

"You like it in this town?"

"The Land of my Fathers."

"You've made my day, boy," he said, "I like it too."

He had called his son 'boy' all his life and had often declared for all to hear that he wasn't going to change the term, however old and gray Bryn might become.

Bryn laughed softly. He loved his little family, so full of affection and 'funny little ways' as his Mam put it.

"How's the hip," Bryn asked.

"My replacement is a treat, don't need a cane any longer, "said the Dad with a chuckle. "I was so lucky, you see. And I don't tire of telling you, or anyone, come to that – the luck of it - just going into the one-pound store to buy my cigarettes, slipped on the steps – crunch! I heard the old hip-bones crack, boy! When I tried to move, it sounded like twigs snapping off a branch. I was in dire straits. Lucky? That store was directly opposite the hospital. They carried me over to the A and E. They operated immediately. In two hours I was outside again, on my way home. Lucky, you see, they'd caught me while I was still warm," he added with a wink, "and I haven't smoked since! One of life's little triumphs, and for once of my own doing!"

Bryn loved the Dad's little stories, and followed him in that tendency.

"I had another funny experience too, Dad. I was walking down by the old estate where they're pulling up the cracked paving stones, and I saw our old neighbour old Mr Smith across the road, he waved to me. I couldn't cross over because of the traffic. I carried on walking. So did he. He suddenly stopped and pointed down at his feet, then at mine. I saw I was standing on the space where a paving stone had been removed. The space had been filled in with cement. I stared and froze. Someone had scrawled letters into the cement which was now solid. Those two letters were 'B J,' my initials, Dad. I was standing on myself. When I looked up, Mr Smith had disappeared. I thought he'd passed away, I think Mam said."

"He did," said the Dad, "there's many a fulfilled genealogy in these parts. It's funny, your story reminds me of when I was in the army. I was an interviewing officer on a WOSB, War Office Selection Board. Our job was to vet the officer cadets to see if they were the right type to go on to be commissioned. Well, one of my fellow officers was Tom Harris, and he asked the candidates just one question. "Describe your uniform, especially the lower garments, like trousers. Yes, say 'trousers.'" We remained straight-faced as the cadets limped through this final crazy test of their competence to become officers. I never saw Tom again for thirty years. Well, I met him at the final Regimental do last month, only time he ever came, and I asked him, "Why did you ask all those cadets to say 'trousers', Tom?" "You can always tell," he said, "'trousers' like that," he pronounced it with a slow, peculiar drawl, "officer material." He then walked out of the Mess, never to return."

"Really?" Bryn managed through the smiles.

"You see, Bryn," the Dad went on, "there are indeed a few answers to some of the pretty crazy questions in our fruitcake life, ones which wise men have found an answer to, but that certainly was not one of them – it was basically, a stray event of nil resolution. We shall never know the truth about Tom's 'trousers.'"

"Tell me, Dad, come on! You know."

"Think on it, boy."

"I will not leave this place in a state of suspended enlightenment, Dad," he declared.

"Oh, yes, you will" the Dad replied, "like the rest of us, and like it."

"Bryn got the point. "Dad if I can ask you one last thing, why is that after looking at me long enough, people sometimes begin throwing stones?"

"Don't worry, boy," he replied "just the inexplicable pebbles of life." He smiled his ironic, comforting smile, a man of fun, kindness and talent. Bryn loved his old Dad.

"Thanks for the messcaffé," he said gesturing at the disgusting liquid stewing in the cups, "I'm off to the books now. Don't be late for dinner. Mam's got your special rice pudding."

Bryn embraced him. The Dad looked him up and down again, this time approvingly, and left. Bryn followed a few moments later. He stood at the worn-out denim and jeans stall in front of the old shell of a school house and watched his Dad out of sight. Everyone he passed, greeted him. The Dad was a much loved man.

He decided on a quick beer before going home and went into the public bar of the awful Rising Sun. The interior was dark, the curtains unwashed, the windows uncleaned, the shelves undusted. It stank as much of urine as yesterday's beer. 'Christ,' he thought, they really should shut this place up.' Although it was market day, there were few customers - a well-dressed, middle-aged woman, with an air of refinement, sat by the window looking out. Her red hair fluffed out, her face free of cosmetics. Bryn wondered what she was doing in this spit-pit of a place. She seemed to be waiting for someone. At a corner table sprawled a dishevelled drunk, his head resting on his arms, snoring lightly, but somehow inoffensively. Another customer, a small, restless, dark creature, simian and vocal, was pacing up and down, occasionally pausing to slap the counter with the heavy metal ring on his finger - 'crack!' There was no sign of anyone behind the bar, except an Alsatian which gave a single bark every time the man hammered on the counter. The door to the back led to some ghastly interior torture chamber no doubt. The apeman now drained his pint, looked around at the comatose, indifferent clientele, and went into a wild harangue: "There are basically only two forms of music, good and evil. The Beatles are good, the Rolling Stones, evil. Left hand, right hand. One evil, one good. Mozart good, Schubert evil. One a family man, the other a syphilitic. Like that. Left, right. I explain that at the station every time, even to the police physician. I have two mistresses, one good one evil. No one has ever seen them. Who am I to say that? Well, here is my passport! "He slapped it down on the counter. "I am privy to many secrets. Look at the last page. It is in German, is it not? This is Adolf Hitler's last testament. Cunning schweinhunt to put it in my passport. No one is aware of this. I speak five languages, so I should know. Write something in my passport. Go on, something good, something evil. 'I love Good, I love Evil,' for example. Beatles, Rolling Stones, Schubert, Mozart. Here!" He abruptly concluded his babble and shouted at the bottles, "half a bitter right now!" The dog at once leapt into life, going for the noisy one, its paws scrabbling on the wooden top, its jowls slavering. The apeman bolted for the door before the beast could get to him. As he rushed out, he nearly bowled over young Geraint, the gentle giant, the family gardener, friend of horticulturists everywhere. Geraint looks down mildly at the precipitate nutcase.

"Hi, Geraint!" Bryn said, still trying to get to grips with good and evil."

"Listen," Geraint said, joining him at the bar, "this morning I went on a quail hunt. In my garden. Cunning, knows all the escape routes that quail, you can see the track lines, holes in the hedge. Never seen one close up before. This time right in the middle, no way out. Beautiful, got a crest, a purple crest. I move forward to grab it. Suddenly it shoots straight up into the air, right up, and flies to the topmost branch and settles down so no one can see him. He sleeps there. Quail lay in their nests, very tiny eggs, very expensive. Well, next moment, I was wandering about, south-west or so of my pond at the bottom of the garden, and I spot an egg in the grass! Kind of pale blue, like a small ceramic bowl. But when I looked closer, I knew, this was not a quail egg, this was a duck egg. I tell you, that bird knows what it's doing, all to put me off its track. I tell you, I've never been so disappointed. "You can eat the egg," Bryn suggested, "No," he said, "I could never do that, I wanted those birds for my little aviary. Then we could all stare at each other and wonder what it's all about. What a disappointment!" The ‘drunk’ woke at this point, stared through sleepy eyes at Geraint, then focused on Bryn. He immediately leapt to his feet, rushed over and began shaking Bryn’s hand vigorously , “Hello there, Fergus, lad!” exclaimed the man excitedly, “Why didn’t you tell us you was coming?” He had a strong Irish brogue and was quite sober. “What you doing over here?”

“I’m sorry to disappoint you,” Bryn said, “I’m not Fergus!”

“But you are Fergus, Fergus Sweeney of County Cork, everyone knows that!”

“Except me,” Bryn said, “ask Geraint here. Do I look like someone else, Geraint?”

“Not that I know of,” said Geraint with quiet conviction. “He’s Bryn Jones of Sir Penfro. I do his Dad’s garden. Honest!”

“The man gaped again at Bryn, “a spitting image! You got a doppelganger on the loose, mate. I’d better pass on the word, OK.”

With a last, long astonished look, he backed out of the front door. As if on cue, the seated lady now came to life, blinked, and began, in turn, to stare at Bryn, wrinkling her brows. She appeared to be trying to remember some distant, forgotten matter. Finally, she moved purposefully across to him, still staring hard, until her face was only an inch away from his. Bryn remained stationary. Where after all, could he go? She suddenly shook her flaming curls and her puzzled expression faded for a moment.

“What in the hall has this day got in store for me now?” Bryn wondered.

“You’ve come for the market, haven’t you?” the woman asked, her voice surprisingly gentle. Bryn nodded. It was true.

“We have many markets here. I don’t think you’ll be disappointed.”

Bryn wondered if she had actually seen any of them.

Her reflective mood softened even more. She reached out and ran her fingers through his hair

"Your hair," she said, "so soft and silky, and falls, see here, in folds like, like the buds of a hyacinth."

"The buds of a hyacinth," repeated Geraint who had been listening intently, "I like it."

A sudden look of realization mixed with rapture spread over her face.

"My God, is it you? You are really one, aren't you?" She seized Bryn's hand," I know who you are!" She pressed his hand against her breast. "Yes, I can feel it, the electricity, like a brand in my heart, the magnetism of the songs of ancient sun-rays rising in me, and I'm not making it up. You are one of the ancient ones, from way back, the eld, come back to greet us over the ages. Can you feel that glow?" she pressed his hand to her breast again, "My God it's running right through me!" She shivered with delight. "Where do you come from? Where?!" she asked, still rapt.

"Carmarthen," he confessed,

"Carmarthen!" I knew it!" she sang out, "Merlin's town! You have come back to tell us. Feel it! I feel it. You have come back to tell us all."

"Yes, yes..." Bryn responded, his words lacking any meaning, but feeling her passion and vision, "Yes, yes, you do," she said, embracing him, holding his hand to her breast again. She finally drew apart, shuddering with pleasure, her face glowing, her eyes shining. He felt her warmth radiate his whole body. She gave him a sighing hug of farewell, kissed him on both cheeks, turned, and in a trice was gone.

Geraint blinked, "Dammo," he exclaimed, "that was a pleasant experience, that was!" and hurriedly followed her out.

Bryn leaned against the bar and thought of the ancient bards, Merlin the Enchanter, and his enigmatic Red-Haired wraiths. Going great, he thought. But when was he going to be served. The dog had now disappeared. And, yes, Geraint was right, it had been a pleasant experience. Bryn slowly moved outside. He found himself gazing at the blooms of the flower stall. The stall-holder was sitting by his dog, a massive mastiff, where do they all come from, he wondered. The hairy hulk was tethered to a lamppost, its huge head lolling from side to side as if about to fall off. For some reason, Bryn felt for his gardening gloves in his pocket. He nodded to the stall holder, who turned away and sipped his char. Quick as a whippet, without any warning, the dog darted forward. Before he could move out of the way, the hound snuffled its snout directly into Bryn's pocket, seized one of the gloves, and retreated behind the lamppost, the gardening gauntlet between its teeth. Bryn moved to retrieve it. The dog shook its hairy locks, snapped at him in warning, then settled down, the glove between its paws. It then proceeded to tear it to pieces, finger by finger, it seemed, glancing at him, as if daring him to act. Bryn stood his ground and gazed, bemused. Even the dogs were now apparently suffering from the universal dementia of the town. When all that remained was a tangled pile of chewed up fabric, the slavering beast stopped masticating and stared up at Bryn. Bryn remained resolutely still. He swore a look of disappointment came into the eyes of the hound. Bryn smiled. He had won. He had not given the dog the satisfaction of losing control and fighting back. He had lost the glove but he had won the war. The stall-holder had looked on through the whole episode with a dead-eye, fish-like expression. He had made no effort to curb the piratical mutt from its plunder or to apologise. Bryn decided he would terminate this savage canine provocation with a suitable, more subtle riposte.

"Here," he said to the stall-holder, "he seems to fancy gloves, so give him this one as well," and handed him the second glove. The stall-holder fondly ruffled the dog's great ugly head, and began feeding the mad beast its second five-fingered feast of the day, fondly watching it chomping and tearing away. Bryn nodded, and moved off. Yes, everything happily concluded, to the satisfaction of all the participants, smiles on their faces, including the dog's.

Bryn suddenly realised he had forgotten his bag of pomegranites somewhere. Should he go back for them? No, he decided - anyway, one of the unbalanced dogs of the town would have probably eaten them by now. He decided to wend his way home through the outskirts of the shrinking town, the abandoned no-man's land where few inhabitants cared to venture. He felt like some watcher of the Lees, a casual overseer of deserted scrublands. The place was dotted with varieties of industrial rot - ruined workshops, collapsed huts, a single smashed railway carriage, the rusting iron skeletons of fallen sheds. Piles of brick-bats and fallen slates and masonry made up the rubble that lay everywhere. He surveyed the seized up pulleys , the smashed security lights, the flattened gates and broken chains, all still in place, vandalized but unstolen. And to tease the mind further, a tumbledown pigeon-loft sunk in a stinking oily pool. Clinker pathways led everywhere and nowhere. Bryn picked his way through the black sacks of kitchen waste, the fat-trap dumps, the stained mattresses and sofas. The surface was spread everywhere with purple mires, troughs, lagoons of oxidising chemicals, leaching from the piles of spoil. He paused as he left the last blasted gateway of the old 'new town' and its blight-lands, and stepped onto the path, leading home. Both sides were lined with blooming clouds of Hawthorn, his and Geraint's favourite floral route to Hendre. The blood-shot alders and elderberry trees, seemed immune to chemical contagion. They were spreading happily over the whole of the toxic meadows. He sniffed the abundant buddleias crowded with cabbage whites, giving off a pervading, fragrant perfume. The ground was covered with yellow ragwort, mayweeds, creeping buttercups, and the ubiquitous cranesbills. They all merged together, all the scents, the colours and the shifting serene images, all brightness and fertility among the buds and blossoms. He stopped to listen to the grasshoppers, the chiff-chaffs, the warblers and song thrushes, especially the greater honey-guide golden oreoles, rare in these parts, friend of the buzzing bee everywhere. He felt the dreadful graveyard with its disintegrating industrial tombstones had again been overshadowed by the simple spots of sunny greenery around him. He felt a rush of pleasure. Yes, even the two-ton, gloomy, pear-shaped inhabitants, must share in it, "nature is generous as well as ubiquitous with its treasures" - the Dad's words; the Red Head happy in her dreams of Merlin; Ben laughing in his tent, canonized once more; Mr Smith back from the dead; Fergus finally laid to rest; Geraint over the moon with the hyacinth; Adolf's last testament finally exposed; all the pets in the world ever so nice; all the stall-holders sharing their cuppa, sullenness banished; even the foul Nescafe joint and the hideous 'Rising', had performed an useful social function; and no more stonings on top of it! Amazing satisfactions all round! As he approached Hendre, the hawthorn bushes seemed to swell up like clouds and burst with all the sweets of paradise. What a day! He strode along, assured that "the subtle magic which is inevitable in the most mystifying scheme of things, has its place even in benighted Pentre Ifan," as the Dad had observed recently. Bryn increased his pace as he thought of home, his Welsh 'Hendre.' His Mam was waiting at the front gate. She hugged him and gave him a big kiss, her eyes shining, "so you're staying a few days longer, Bryn. Lovely." She took his arm and led him indoors.

"Did you have a good day?"

"Just... about normal, Mam."

"Have you decided on a name for it yet?"

"Got a bit of a choice, 'The Day of the Ancient Bard,' 'The Day of the Torn Gauntlet' or 'The Day of the Quail,' which one, Mam?"

"We've used 'bard' before, I don't know about 'gauntlet', so, - 'The Day of the Quail.'"

“So be it then!”

“Now, love, come and have some of my nice rice pudding before your Dad eats it all up.”

The Hair Dryer

Gareth had bought one of the terrace cottages of the deserted derelict railway station just outside Cardiff. Where fifteen trains a day used to go to the southern Welsh metropolis, now there was only one rickety old bus per day. The domestic buildings were surrounded by a wasteland of various grasses, rosebay willow herb with its striking scarlet blossoms, yellow curling vetches, standing stalks of common sorrel, carpets of white yarrow and knot grass, all of which blanketed the uncleared stone chips of the line, the discarded blackened cross ties and the piles of Victorian red-brick rubble. Among the clovers of the southern boundary, the pale shoots of the dreaded Japanese knotweed were already threatening to take over. It was a desolate space, teeming with wild life, and sounded only with the winds of the day and the trills of the blackbirds and song thrushes in the wide stretches of buddleia, dotted with darting and wheeling cabbage whites. The floating fruit seeds of the willows, hazels and alders were diffused in the early summer glow, and gave it a misty magical hue. The whole place was normally devoid of human movement. That was why Gareth had, rather impulsively, chosen to spend his savings on one of the solid now neglected station houses. But up at Number one, the first of the row of five, stirred, yes, the familiar figure of the ominous human. Gareth was approaching from the front of the building so he couldn't avoid his detested new neighbour. Ray had bought one of the cottages 'as an investment,' so his garden was thick with nettles and brambles. All the window frames and doors remained cracked and peeling. "Do the garden and stuff when the prices go up," he had assured Gareth. "Yes," he had confided, "the Council's got big plans for this whole space, buy in now, that's what I'm doing." They met outside Number One. Gareth noted that the stupid hair dryer with it astronaut-like domed helmet still stood erect in the bay window - as bright and grotesque as the day it was born, no doubt. He detected a slight movement there. Jesus, was there now an actual inhabitant within?

"I'm Ray Davies," Ray had introduced himself a few weeks before, "Weights and Measures."

"Sorry...?" Gareth had queried.

"Ray. Me. Weights and Measures. Ref yr query, City Council, here too, on the boundary, like I told you. You have to have permission from there for here. Not my department but I get around, got a pal or two here and there."

Gareth had wanted planning permission for an extension. When they had discovered that they were neighbours, Ray had been arch, coy, elusive, as if he could help, but 'it's the time, see, boyo,' he had sighed, 'haven't got none to spare. But, like I said, I mean, your application, bottom of the pile. Yes, I seen it," he said in hushed tones as if he had observed Moses' burning bush, "but it's not like what you said, Gareth, remember, ' 'money talks,' you said, that was a laugh, ha ha! - it's just fodder, to oil the wheels like. Two brown envelopes, see, one hundred for my colleague, one hundred for me. Then your file at the bottom will rise overnight like a mushroom to the very top. Stamped first thing in the morning, APPROVED! You'd save, we'd save, my property would go up in value too, a grant for me as well, everyone's happy. I mean everyone does it. I know you left it hanging, dammo, I even told my superior that you was not a man to be trifled with, not to approach you till I carried out preliminary searches, so there's be no contraytemps, like, later, see. So, Gareth boyo, don't say nothing till next time. Then tell me, and tell me it's – YES - definite like!" He winked, "and you got to keep your new missus happy - takes hard-shit cash, boyo!"

Ray had a broad Cardiff accent with an Easter Ender TV overlay, both hideous cadences. His spoke the old Tiger Bay jargon which was sometimes incomprehensible. But the timbre of his voice was something else. He seemed to speak in layers of silk, each phrase slipping out like a tongue to lick the listener into a state of sensual ease. Whatever the rubbish he spoke, that lingual promise of overall ecstasy was never far away. His round face and soft creamy skin, were appealing as a baby's. His green eyes conveyed a look of sincerity, innocence and unbridled lust, a contrary and incandescent mix.

"Yes," he went on, "as I was saying last time, girls love that magic taste of mine. Born with it I was. Look at my skin. See, like powdered dough before it goes into the oven, like goose down, feel the texture," he stroked his cheeks and his bare arm. His skin seemed to give out a white cloud of miniscule sweet-smelling spoors, leaving finger-tip tracks in the velvet. He hurried on, glorying in the sensational gifts he had been blessed with. "And then, a few words of the warm syrup, and they're down there on the bed, legs apart, like that. Irresistable. See, I was going to see the sex shows at Amsterdam and I got talking to this Dutch girl on the ferry. Anyway I could tell by the way she was quivering that it was on. She worked in the docks and had a flat nearby. Well, I tell you, as soon as I was inside, we stripped off, and I began licking her all over, using my feathery sixty-nine non-stop procedure, boyo, the whole lot. In seconds, she begins grunting, writhin'. Then on with my milky-way technique, not technique really, just comes natural, with all my smoothy drip-drops, like, down there, between her labials, up and down, then across and across, flat tongue open, tight tongue closed, juicy as hell in a minute. Then like the flight of a pigeon, she goes into a long hump-grunting orgasm, like a bloody snake rearing its head, the rest threshing around, all glistening with sweat and cunt juices, I can tell you. Breathless she was, clung to me like ivy. Wheeeee! Then she gasps out loud, 'you're my man, you're my magic silkman, the man with a touch of velvet and a tongue like a peach!" Wheeeeee? Where'd she get all that? I tell you. Said it was the best come she'd ever had, "Thought my brains was going to explode and my tits and cunt fly across the room in pieces!" Hear that! And now every other weekend she sends me a ticket, and I travel down to her place. For free. As soon as the door opens, she grabs me and says "my Mister Magic Silkman! Come here my Mister Magic!" She unzips me, flips out my cock, and goes down on me, right on the door step, then drags me by my cock to the bed. But I lick her back, like a threshing machine and she's flopping round like a fish on a slab again. This time I really did think she had blown up, internal like. After all them frantic earth movements, boyo, she got stiff as a poker and clung onto me like a limpet. It was ages before she cooled off - but then it was like a blower fish all over again." He exhaled with immense satisfaction. "Well, that's what I can do. Every two weeks now, a free trip to Amsterdam. And I tell you, I'm not only Mr Magic Silkman for little Miss Tulip, I'm Mr Magic Silkman all over here. All over the office. True. Word's got around. Never know how. What do you think of that?"

Before Gareth could think of a reply to Ray's narcissistic, squalid but compulsive drivel, Ray's eyes focused on Gareth's front door farther down. He'd spotted Gareth's new wife, Michelle, with an expert eye, as she came out to hang up the washing. The washing was always hung out in the front here, as if celebrating a great, endless imperial triumph. Ray winked roguishly at Gareth as she went back into the house. Michelle gave them a teasing sexy farewell wave of the hand. Ray grunted ecstatically and nudged Gareth. "Got to keep 'em happy!" He lowered his voice. "Look, if you're ever a bit short," he paused, "you know, the old brewers' droop and all that, call me in to do the honours, your fastest local silkman in the west! She won't be disappointed, I promise you." He guffawed again. Gareth pointed at Ray's upper right cheek bone.

"What's the bruise you've got there, Ray. How did that happen? Got the makings of a great black eye."

"Bloody cunt!" Ray suddenly burst out, "so I'd had his wife once or twice, my colleague in Weights and Measures, but it wasn't serious, and I got this," he indicated his bad eye, "because I was sitting down. A lucky punch on my face. Then he nearly tore off my bloody ear. Look, see," he winced as he stretched out his right ear, with a scab just beginning to form at the join. "The swine. If he hadn't caught me on the hop sitting down, I'd have done him serious damage, boyo!" he fingered his ear gently. "Win some, lose some, I know, yes, but only because I was sitting down, the swine!"

The front door of Ray's house suddenly burst open and Ray's latest girl friend hurried out. Gareth had seen her a couple of times before. 'Rita' was unmistakable – short, well-endowed with fatty tissue, but still shapely, with bouncing breasts, and a rushed, excitable manner which made her flesh shiver and shake, a perfect companion to Ray's hectic velvet underground. She exuded all the perfumes of Araby, a bountiful stink. Her abundant ginger hair was dyed and done up into tight curls and looked almost mechanically rigid, fresh from the astronaut's helmet in the window, no doubt. Her whole head shone like a swarm of blue-bottles on a cow pat. She patted the cultivated curls into place and smiled at Gareth. She caught his responding grin, jiggled her hips and smiled back. Ray scowled, took her by the hand and kissed it, tongue first. True to Ray's word, she went at once into lover mode, sort of shuddering, moaning, almost protestingly, her mouth opening, lips immediately moist.

"Dammo!" she growled impatiently, "I got to meet him now. With Ma-in-law. Can't get out of it. See you afterwards. I'll think of something, my Silkman, and you know how!" She embraced him tightly, made like a cat, 'ggrrawww!' moaned again and flounced up the road to her Volkwagon and drove off with a screech of tyres.

"Well, there goes my goer, I told you didn't I!?"

"You been licking her off for long?"

"Why you ask?"

"I mean, you're her 'Mister Magic Silkman.'"

"You're right there."

"Just wondered."

"Notice her fingers did you?"

"As a matter of fact, I didn't. Why?"

"The ring, the big wedding ring, the big engagement diamond on the next finger, and a gold bangle on top. Her husband. Number one architect. Tons of moolah. And a nympho in bed, but nothing like my Dutch bitch. I only been fuckin' Rita snce she came back from her honeymoon. But crisis! Yesterday she called her old man, 'Ray,' she told me, just slipped out. He went wild, but she got round him, she always does. That's why I got that hair dryer in there. Goes back home to hubby and all she has to say is, "look at my new hair-do, took all afternoon, suits me, don't you think?" Then he's all over her. Believe anything, the twat. That's why I bought that machine, see, in the first place, a perfect cover. Christ, we have a laugh. But we've decided to take a little rest, whew! – till next time!" He guffawed and dug Gareth in the ribs again. "Now, to business, what about that permission for the extension?" he rubbed finger and thumb together, "the crinkly browns." He chuckled, expecting agreement.

"I think I'll be sticking with my solicitor," Gareth said slowly. Ray's pale, round face was momentarily transfixed by the word, 'solicitor.'

"You sure?" he asked tentatively.

"There'll be no 'contraytemps,' I assure you, Ray."

"Have it your way then. But no hard feelings." He turned to go, "Give my best to lovely Michelle, won't you, boyo."

"I will. And a great idea for you and Rita to take a 'rest,' too, Ray."

"Why's that then?"

"Well, you don't want another shiner, do you?"

Ray nervously felt his ear, and, for once, fell silent. He turned for home.

Gareth strode out into the centre of the wasteland. He stopped knee-high in the marvellous spreading bunches of weeds and looked around. He glanced up as a sudden gust of wind ruffled the tops of the wild flowers. A cloudy highly perfumed silvery miasma seemed to rise and settle over the leaves and the bees of the place. Gareth examined every footstep he had taken to get as far as this, and, looking around again, wondered how long it would all last.

The Last Supper

Dense layers of inky clouds were building up in the wintry sky. It would be preternaturally dark and even more intolerably miserable in half an hour - a fitting cap to an unbearable day. "A graveyard," Patrick muttered. He paused at the door of number 111, key in one hand, carrier bag of groceries in the other. Was this his last day at the house? He loved the place, it had been his and Teresa's ever since they had decided to live together. It was her property, no doubt of that, but - no Will. Would her poisonous siblings, brother William and his ugly spinster sisters, Felicity and Fay, now kick him out of 111. "No Will, no home," William had warned him. The ghastly triumvirate were desperate to sell up the old homestead and depart again for more fun holidays in the sun. Their own large house stood close to the centre of the small town, five minutes walk farther up. It belonged to the family. Teresa had deeded it to her siblings, hoping it would diminish their greed, but it had merely amplified it. They pursued her to the end, even to her death-bed; in her last agony, she had managed to whisper something to Patrick as he bent over her. William, straining his ears behind him, had given a grunt of anger. Patrick saw only Teresa's gentle unafraid smile fading before his eyes. He suppressed a sob. "'Taken care?'" had she said? "What else?" He spoke softly, "there is no Will, love," and shivered.

He stared blankly at the front door. Dare he go back inside? Teresa had been the love of his life; she was sixty-seven when she died, he thirty-five. There had never been any problem about that. They were both slender and fit from all the exercise they took, Teresa with a youthful granny look, Patrick with a sprinkling of gray, but no lines, laughter or otherwise. A handsome pair! They doted on each other, their shared interests, the cooking, gardening, the wine cellar, the art, painting, poetry, the renovations - they had practically laid out the garden hand in hand, a couple born to be together. Ben they had both loved equally and he, them. Age difference? No time for that! That was why they never married. Then, gradually, she became breathless after each little chore, but insisted she "never felt better " – which was true. But now, Teresa's healing work was done.

Patrick had been one of Ben's patients. Ben and Teresa, husband and wife, both doctors, had run a private clinic all their professional lives. Patrick was first invited for weekends. In a few months they had become a ménage á trois, but without the sex. When Ben died, Patrick had helped her through her grief and she, his. It was then she had persuaded Patrick to give up his day job as a part-time teacher, live together at the week-end house in the small Welsh town of Pentre Ifan, and do the renovations full-time. Each would care for the other in constant companionship. That was the idea, and so it had worked out. With Teresa's money, they were well set up. 'Happiest time of our lives,' Patrick murmured to himself, 'no doubt of it.' But what about the deadly trio?

When William had learned that Teresa and Patrick had moved into the town, he lost it completely. He cursed the day she was born and paced up and down in his spacious living room wishing she was dead. His unmarried sisters, Fay and Felicity, looked on nervously, nodding agreement to every grimy accusation. "Here! This very spot. Never warned us either." He poured himself another drink. He was short, fat with flapping dewlaps, a rosy nose distended with burst whisky veins. He occasionally hammered on the table to make a noisy point. "Shame on the greedy ageing whore! Her and her disgusting toy boy! They've ruined their reputations, I'll see to that, but they will never deny me my inheritance! And she's sixty-seven if she's a day, and peaky with it." William glared around. His eyes held a permanent wary, shifty expression, mixed with suspicion, greed , and fear. He was capable of doing anything in his own interests. Futile outbursts of bullying and loud empty threats were the music of the household. William was a retired auctioneer and had never left his hectoring habits behind.

Felicity tried to interrupt, "... but Teresa said..."

William cut her off, "I know she promised we'd have 'our fair share of the estate,' but what's 'fair' to a diseased mind? And this house has always morally been mine." He banged his fist on the table. "Don't you worry, I know what's going on. They might appear to be respectable from the outside But I tell you, inside, the devil himself is raging, goading him on to do his worst! Even now, that felon is working on our poor benighted sister, driving her into premature senility, mental and physical. And still no Will!" he pointed accusingly at them.

"We've searched every nook and cranny, William, dear, including the flower pots on the terrace..." ventured Fay.

"...those two sinners spent a suspiciously long time there," put it Felicity, in support – a mistake. William banged his fist on the table again, silencing her.

"But no recognised legal document! Total blank." He resembled a swollen, rolled up spitting rattlesnake, its fangs bared, ready to strike. The sisters recognised the danger and compressed their lips in silence. "For God's sake, wimmin, get moving, find that Will! Your last chance!"

Patrick looked over the enchanted building, their old home, two end-houses of an old Victorian row. They had done up the houses bit by bit, converting the two front doors into a single entrance. Inside, they had enlarged the rooms laterally, so that the ground floor formed a wide two-way extension; to the left, an open kitchen with the dining table where they had cooked their gourmet meals, often with the rays of the setting sun streaming in through the garden windows, illuminating the steaming dishes. Patrick had already prepared the ingredients for a 'last supper,' as requested, now ready for the final touches. The space to the right was for lounging in, with drinks cabinet, TV, radio and disc player and piles of DIY mags.

At the back was the recently added conservatory, with a curtain to conceal the alcove. There were other doors to the left and right and a spacious garden at the back. These doors were never locked. William and his hideous cohorts, the carrion crows, Fay and Felicity, carried out their furtive explorations only when Teresa and Patrick were away. William, once again, gritted his teeth, knocked back his drink, and yelled for them to 'pull their fingers out!" He widened the scope of his own intrusive enquiries, called on his neighbours, the banks, the town's two solicitors' offices and his own chief adviser, Mr Abel Evans of Evans and Evans. Not a shred of a will emerged, not even in 111's herbaceous borders, he thought grimly. William had also been appalled to observe that the townspeople didn't seem to mind the odd couple. In fact they appeared to approve of the union, and could tell him nothing. But Mr Evans remained faithful to the cause and urged them on to further frantic treasure hunts.

Then after months of full of happy days working on the improvements, Teresa had suddenly collapsed. Patrick felt himself propelled into uncontrollable nightmare, the final shade had fallen. He knew this was the end for her. Now he had to face up to it. He made her comfortable on the sofa by the kitchen, his hands shaking, his mouth dry - her loving carer to the end. William and his sisters arrived almost immediately, as if informed by some invisible bush telegraph. William and the two crows waited by her death-bed, hands clasped in prayer, dabbing at dry eyes with barely concealed expressions of exultation. Teresa's life slowly flickered out. Patrick beheld the coming void with the silence of a statue. He leaned over her, sensing her last words, William heard the whisper too and started back, shocked. 'Taken care of...last supper...'!? This could mean only one thing – Conspiracy! He stared at the dying face in disbelief. He had been right all along. Teresa'a gaze gently settled on Patrick, she moaned just once, exhaled imperceptibly, her eyelids drooped, her features sagged, then stilled utterly - she had made her final farewell.

'At last!" breathed William. Patrick was momentarily frozen, speechless. William glanced at him angrily. What had Patrick done to bring on his sister's unexpected death? An 'infractus' or something, he had heard later. But what did that really mean? And what had the swine done with the Will? Patrick remained, hands clasped, on his knees by her side, his chest heaving in silent, countless paroxysms of grief.

William seized the opportunity, "Home now!" he ordered the sniffling sisters, ushering them out, "leave the arrangements to me!" he shouted in farewell, "Mr Evans has my instructions."

When William arrived home, his words spilled out in a never-ending foul-tempered stream. He paused to open a new bottle and gulped down two greedy swallows of Johnny Walker. His two familiars began to sob uncontrollably, as if their purses would break. There had been, after all, a death in the family, however unpleasant the deceased. "We just wanted something to cherish her by her," Fanny sighed. Fay managed a little sob of agreement, "not just the Will..." She looked at brother William, striding up and down, the very picture of the master huntsman exercising his ancient rights. "Conspiracy!" he bellowed every so often. "Abel Evans is the best solicitor in the County and he confirmed it! – but this intrigue don't wash with me! I am up to it, Mr Evan's advice is expert! I am next of kin, the eldest! The estate belongs to me." He thumped his chest, "I, William, her brother, next of kin, the eldest, with all the prerogatives that go with that! No plot can touch me!" he repeated furiously, beginning to slur his words, "the rightful heir, incontestable! I can chuck anyone out of my property whenever I so wish. I can confiscate anything here, even that onyx ashtray!" He pointed at the inoffensive article. "And I will exercise my prerogative this very day. It is my responsibility to clean up this swamp of immorality, this den of thieves, these vile plots! For confirmation, you will listen to Evans the solicitor himself, right now! Come on!"

Together, for the umpteenth time, they hurried to Abel Evans's rooms in town. Mr Evans settled them down, chalked up the fees, opened the proceedings, repeated the same old obfuscating legal guff, knowing their greed would keep them coming, and pay his ever fattening expenses - and then pressed on to deal with more important questions, "William, on your last visit, you said that - I mean, got to be straight - you heard it said that where 'there was no Will, there was no money'" Right? Well, not true, William, there's always plenty of money to be made out of intestate cases, don't you worry, it'll work out in your favour one hundred per cent while I'm here on this earth!"

"That's the spirit!" declared William, glaring at his mute, intimidated sisters. "As to the conspiracy..."

"I've told you, "Mr Evans admonished mildly, "...leave that to me," Mr Evans was quite clear on this point. William's paranoid fantasy had to be controlled, otherwise the sisters might well turn on their brother, how they loathed him! - declare him incompetent even, which he undoubtedly was, thereby deferring the payment of his own quite legitimate profits, "So, calmly now, forget it, William. Now as to your sister's properties and investments" He tapped a pile of documents in front of him on his desk. "Your sister's Estate! Oh, she's been quite open about her holdings, it's just there's been no will, as yet, but that's no surprise, a minor point... now look at her holdings in Sainsbury's alone, the grocery shop...look!" The group settled down to do the sums, the three siblings growing more and more excited, and Mr Abel Evans, of Evans and Evans, more and more rich.

Patrick looked up. The moon was shone among the louring clouds and a shrill, chill, wind swept over him. Patrick clutched his bag. Had all that dying and money-grubbing been but this very same day? Where was he going now? He held his breath. With an abrupt movement, he turned the key, and stepped inside.

A single table-lamp lit the room. He glanced around - books, papers, the table still as he had set it for dinner - nothing disturbed, - yes, they had been careful again - the alcove curtain still drawn. He remained fixed to the spot. A heavy black cloak seemed to envelope him. He groped forward, his chest heaving. He blinked back tears. Teresa! Teresa! God, how insupportable it all was. Just today, the unspeakable William, and was this to last him all his life? How to tidy it all away? What to do about the awful anguish? Again, he stifled a sob. He had to keep control - for Teresa, her last request. He looked at the row of cookery books on the sideboard, they had been collected from every part of the globe, from rare Thai fish dishes to superheated Mexican con carne's. Piles of torn out menus were piled up, carefully collected over the years, some crammed into files, some covered with grease spot and hastily scribbled culinary instructions. The whole story of their life together was here, he thought. He had left the oven plates on low. All the ingredients were gently bubbling in the copper saucepans. He took the parsley and thyme from the bag and neatly chopped them up. He was cooking their fabulous pasta dish, their old favourite, a Tuscan ravioli, with the pork filling finely shredded, with not a fragment of lard in it, aromatic with the mixed herbs of Provence - a recipé they had used a hundred times. It was also Teresa's last whispered request. Why? he wondered again. And now, the final touch. He held the pepper grater, and paused - now only to add...was it *black* pepper? Or *brown*? He paused. He always got it wrong, but Teresa had always been there to help him. Damn, he had to get this right. He ruffled quickly through the old menus looking for the one in red biro, the Tuscan recipe, then paused, overcome again. The bottle of wine was open and stood on the sideboard, ready at room temperature. He steeled himself again, sniffed the cork, poured out a glass, a superb Chateuau Neuf du Pape, their favourite, filled a second glass and placed it at Teresa's place at the table.

The back door to the left was abruptly shoved open and William stepped inside. He paused when he saw the thieving madman, Patrick, standing by the oven. William sniffed, and recoiled. That stinking foreign muck again! And what was the bastard doing, cooking at a time like this? Patrick caught the grimace of disgust on William's face. He saw the swine was drunk as usual.

"I been talking!" William declared with a wave of the hand, "the solicitor said you should pay half the funeral and the tombstone expenses. Two thousand five hundred pounds, with twenty words on the stone thrown in with a discount."

"I've been to the funeral parlour too," Pat said evenly "and the cost on my side amounts to two hundred pounds. The tombstone only costs five hundred, and the twenty words are for free."

"Hell," William thought, " dirty, sly sod, better go carefully, so soon after Teresa'a death too!" He shifted uneasily.

"But the residue of the entire estate, Mr Evans is most insistent, and in law, too, belongs to me, next of kin! I have every right to tell you to bugger off."

"I'm staying on for a while..."

"...without a Will," William, brayed, "don't you understand you haven't a leg to stand on, so I'm giving you notice to quit as from now!"

"You've searched every 'nook and cranny' as your sisters claim, and there is no will."

"Teresa said the estate would go to her family, Fay, Felicity, me."

"You have a fine house up there, plus half her investments.

"Fair's fair," blustered William. "Family! As to the low-down conspiracies over price, Mr Abel Evans, my solicitor will see to the real costs you will have to pay, and to your situation here, which is illegal!"

"Please don't interrupt me while I'm preparing food."

"How dare you actually cook at a time like this?"

"Staying on for a while, I said," said Patrick , looking at the alcove. William's eyes widened with a dawning horrified understanding, "No!

As arranged, that's the law, " he stuttered, "you have taken her to the funeral parlour, haven't you?"

"Teresa's wish was for a last supper, that's law too."

"Sacrilege!"

"You heard her."

"She was out of her head, demented."

Pat crossed over to and pulled back the curtain. On a trellis, stood Teresa's coffin. It was constructed of woven boughs of osier and crack willow, still in leaf, intertwined with fresh wild primroses, violets and daffodils. The top was open and Teresa lay there in her flower bed, still and calm, a serene smile on her face.

"What in the hell is going on now?" demanded William stepping back in fear, bafflement and some trepidation. What was the devil up to?

"Her last resting place, her last supper, as requested."

"This is going straight to Abel Evans," said William, bunching his fists. He marched to the coffin, bent over, gripped the top end and pulled violently. Pat seized the other and held on. William tugged, stumbled and fell, the coffin tipping to the floor. William tried to grip it again. At that instant, with Teresa looking on, the wine poured, her feast prepared, Pat realized that he was perfectly capable of killing a fellow human being. He advanced on the creature on the floor as it scrambled towards the back door. William had seen the look in Patrick's eye and knew it was time to leave, whatever the fate of the corpse.

"Your last supper!" the roused reptile shouted, pointing tremblingly at the table,

"you wait, you madman! Your last supper!"

He fell out of the door and the shadows closed in after him. Patrick relaxed, at least one less devil out of it. He righted the trestle and wheeled Teresa over to the table, manoeuvring her so that her head stood just opposite her place. He glanced at the gently bubbling utensils, "but the last touch, which is it, my love, I always forget, is it the *brown* or the *black* pepper?" he asked, searching through the menus, tears coursing down his cheeks. He picked up a loose bulky envelope, the torn flap exposing the brown cover inside with instructions in red biro, and the hand-writing heartrendingly familiar - Teresa's! He hurriedly read the title words, gasped and swayed, "This is the last Will and testament of I, Teresa..." The Will itself! He glanced down at the shelf, there, all the time, like herself, hidden in plain view! She knew he would have to consult their old menus for the last supper. Patrick leaned weakly against the edge of the table, steadied himself, then laid out the documents, - there were three copies of the Will, the first one, the original, for Patrick, his name on the outside, one for Mr Evans of Evans and Evans, and one for William and his sisters. He turned the cover and read, "...to my dear life's companion, Patrick Heath, I bequeath the tenancy of 111...this property is to revert to William, my brother, or my sisters, Fay and Felicity, should the said Patrick predecease them. Also... one third of all the profits and incomes...from my remaining investments, to the aforementioned Patrick...shall them enjoy for as long as he shall live..." 'Taken care!' this was it! He realised the will was so made that it could not be challenged. Whatever happened to him, a large proportion would still go to the family! Patrick dipped his finger into Teresa's wine and leaned over the coffin. He placed his finger on Teresa's lips so the wine ran down into her mouth. "To you, my love, as promised, a last supper, and a last Will!" He breathed again, in joy, relief, - and grief. 111 was still his home! His tears ceased. Now to the Last Supper, he sniffed the pasta, their common final feast - yes, it needed pepper, *black* pepper! He grated it over the simmering ravioli. Yes, the dish was now ready. He sipped his glass and raised it in farewell to Teresa. Later that same night, when the moon had opened fair and bright, from that toast onwards, Patrick treasured the memory of his beloved Teresa being there to share in the finest dishes they had ever prepared together.

Dialogues with Gerald

The following short stories are in commemoration of my dear friend the late Gerald Meylan of the Canton de Vaud, Switzerland, and of the many agreeable moments we spent over a glass of the best Vaudois wines.

‘Where have all the Monarchs Gone?’

I was sitting at a table in the Bishop’s café by the Cathedral, with Gerald, my (teaching) mate, (off duty) and colleague (on duty.)

“Cheers to your English monarchs then!” said Gerald, always interested in the incredible story of royal England.

“Gerald” I said “there are really no English kings.” “What about William the Conqueror 1066? Everyone knows him, even in the Canton de Vaud.”

“Never Willy the Cónq!” I explained, “a Viking-Norman who spoke hardly a word of English and an absolute bastard, in fact as well as in law! Nor his son either, red-haired Rufus, a homosexualist, assassinated in the New Forest. Nor his grandson either, Henry of Anjou who married Eleanor of Aquitaine, nor their children, called the ‘Plantagenets’ (from the French flower, génestè) or ‘the devil’s brood’ (from the people.) Firstly, John the Wicked, the ‘Butcher of the Irish; then another homosexualist, Richard the Lionheart, an ex-con who spent only a few months of his life in England and the rest in jail. Where’s the English there? Nor later, Gerald, Edward I ‘Hammer of the Scots’ either, or his son Edward II, homosexualist extraordinaire again, ‘assassinated by having a hollow tube shoved up his rectum and a white-hot poker inserted therein so his murdered body would reveal no external wounds.’ Not very English! Who next? Yes, Edward III, ‘Slaughterer of the French’, who also tried to persuade the English Parliament to speak English. And failed, until poet Chaucer did the job for him. Or Henry V, victor of Agincourt, whose body was boiled down and only his fat buried in England? Or the last Norman-Angevin-Acquitanian-Plantagenet the hunchbacked Richard III, (“My kingdom for a horse!”) killed at the battle of Bosworth by Henry VII, son of a Welsh Squire who had seduced Henry V’s French widow, Catherine, of the noble French Valois line. Or Welsh Henry VII’s son, Henry VIII, a brilliant syphilitic, star-chamber tyrant, or his daughter, the red-haired Welsh-speaking Elizabeth, a questionable virgin, surely? And when she died, who came next? A Scot! James VI of Scotland, a bandy-legged, stubborn homosexualist again, father of Charles 1 who had his head cut off by Oliver Cromwell in one of the few acts of common sense in English history. Or his son, the Scot James II kicked out of England in 1688 for spiritual deviations? Who next? Yes, William of Orange, yes, homosexualist of the Dutch Royal house. And when that nationality didn't work, another cousin, fiftieth in line, German George I of Hanover who spoke not a word of English, followed by his son George II who spoke even less, and then their son, George III, a good father and raving lunatic who once got out of his carriage in Windsor Park and addressed an oak tree as 'Emperor of Prussia?' Or his son, George IV, one of the most debauched and delightful men of his age, whose divorced wife beat on the doors of Westminster Abbey when her husband was being crowned, demanding to be made Queen of the – 'English'? When the Hanoverian line failed, another German cousin, Victoria of Saxe-Coberg, a lady who, warned by 'her doctor of a difficult accouchement, pleaded, "it won't stop me still having fun in bed with Albert her Consort, equipped with a strong German accent and a brilliant education,– yes – and enthroned for the rest of the century. And, later her corpulent son Edward VII, 'sexy Eddie,' a slave to the ecstasy of Parisian sex machines, who was addicted, as his mother was, to the highly fashionable 'cocaine wine' of Angelo Moriani of, Paris. Then good King George, and after him, who next? Who next? Yes, Edward. VIII, later Duke von Windsor, who gave up the throne simply because his tiny (miniscule) penis could only be aroused by the knowing couch techniques of twice divorced Mrs Simpson. ('Bravo duchesse! You put some lead in his pencil!' as a wit of the time exclaimed.) Yes, Eddie deserves his place in history the only monarch in the world who gave up his Kingdom for an erection. And why not? Cheers, Eddie! To the present Queen, whose total mediocrity of mind is redeemed only by her gigantic avarice? No! To the last item then, pathetic Charles, son of the mongrel Elizabeth II who wed the Greek-German Prince, Phillip von Battenberg? No. so you see, Gerald, no English Kings mentioned anywhere. But of course there was a last English king. I'll tell you - Harold I, finished off by William the Bastard in 1066, with a Norman arrow stuck in his eye, flat out, as on the Bayeux tapestry. So drink to the last Saxon king, Gerald, Harold the Eyeless, poor fellow, and not a native monarch since - perhaps the English are saving up!- as Napoleon put it 'with perfide Albion, you never know!" Prosit, Gerald!

England, Land of Royal Ceremonies

Today, I showed my mate, Gerald de Vaud, my favourite framed portrait of our wonderful Queen. We were sitting with her at a table at our usual Bishop's café. "She is shown here," I tapped the portrait, "presiding over her 'Maundy' ceremony on the steps of St Paul's Cathedral." Gerald looked a little puzzled.

"In England," I explained, "we make a ceremony out of everything and our wonderful Queen is usually at the centre of them. See her here, the wealthiest woman in the world, handing out token mediaeval farthings (the 'Maunday money') to poverty-stricken old age pensioners once a year, and the whole of England applauds!"

Gerald was plainly astonished by the arithmetic involved in calculating the Queen's fortune, as well as by her ceremonies, "Mon dieu!" he declared!

"Yes," I continued "England has become the world centre of every useless hypocritical ceremony ever invented. But never mind, as long as it looks good. The facade, especially of royalty, is everything! But let's set aside the pathetic gestures reserved for the delectation of the poor. Look to all our royal-blood Jubilees, the silver, gold and diamond weddings, for example, with tons of bells ringing and gifts pouring in from presidents and Arabian mobsters, to name but a few. And, for the more modern eye, TV spectaculars of our royal honeymooners, with their undertones of leisurely copulations and irresistible ejaculations by divine right! And loads of drivel too about nasty fallings out of love and unhealthy divorces, not good for the nation. But there are other far more humble events at the Court of St James to comfort the citizenry - the daily investitures of the Royal Order of St Michael, for example, of St George and of the Most Noble Order of the Bath, and for sundry baronetscies, viscountancies, rare marquisates and common or garden peerages. But on a more informal note, there are also Palace

Receptions for incoming and outgoing Field Marshals, Ambassadors, Gentlemen-in-Waiting, Ladies-in-Waiting, Aidesde camp, Equerries, Military Attaches, all of which are gazetted too, to make everyone who missed a title, agonizingly jealous. And on a wider canvass, we have Military Tatoos, Triumphal Royal Air Force Fly Pasts, Regimental March Pasts, Fleet Reviews with one-thousand gun salutes, and the fabulous Trooping of the Colour to celebrate the Sovereign's birthday - three thousand immense Royal Coldstream Guardsmen drawn up in tight formation - and not a fart between them, such is English discipline! Then we have the commemoration of our glorious war dead in Whitehall at the 'Cenotaph', an immense pile of stained concrete blocks, where all the royals remember our fallen heroes for two minutes of enforced silence, with poppies. (Perhaps two minutes of rage at the criminal donkeys who caused the slaughter might be more appropriate.) Then we have the mile-long scarlet and purple ermine processions of the one-thousand or so hereditary Peers of our House of Lords! And our Lords Spiritual in their silken finery would be the envy any College of Cardinals in Rome in full techicolour! Yes, we crown a ceremony for every mindless, useless occasion. Look at our most recent rituals for royal visits to the British Army Equipment Exhibition, the British Knitting and Clothing Extravaganza, the International Velocity's Royal Cycle Safety Prize giving! Now, Gerald, look at this last lovely simple global example of queenly ceremony, the world's number one tennis players all bowing and curtsying to a' box' at Wimbledàn again with divine right written all over it. All this to the applause and participation of foreigners from all over the globe. Miraculous! That's how much the world loves our royals! Look, Gerald," I urged him, "wouldn't Suisse-Romand love to have a taste of our marvelous Queen? For just a day? You could borrow her, you know. You'd have to pay, she doesn't come cheap. But she's good at it, she was Queen of Africa and Empress of India in her day, so she could manage a canton or two before breakfast, 'Queen of the Kingdom of Vaud!' A real Queen on your coins at last, just for a few hours? Go on, admit it, you'd love it!"

Gerald fell strangely silent, then in a sort of fit, he grabbed my superb portrait of Liz II. “No!” I struggled, “give it back! The Canton of Vaud shall never have this radiant Queen! Find your own! I wish I’d never shown her to you in the first place!”

I just managed retain my priceless framed portrait of the Queen. But we soon returned to our former bonhomies and toasted just about everybody, living and dead, royalty and peasantry! What a good Swiss wine will do!

Later, I had a stray horrible thought, quite inadvertent I assure you, did Gerald de Vaud in his fit of mania, actually try to damage by wrenching my portrait of our gracious Queen, not merely to possess it, which was quite understandable, but dent it? No! I dismissed this half-drunken fantasy at once as too grotesque, too blasphemous, too anti-Christ even!

So, I can say with Wimbledon and the rest of the world, (especially the canton de Vaud!) ‘God bless our Queen’s super ceremonies and all who sail in them!”

The_Uniform Culture_of England

I was sitting at our accustomed table at the Cafe Eveche with my friend Gerald de Vaud *watching* the pupils coming and going from the College opposite

"Do you realize, Gerald" I observed "that in England at this very moment at least eight million school children like these, from six to eighteen are also going to school - but with this difference, every one of them is in sexy uniforms, uniforms of all colours, combinations of purples, greens, yellows, uni-coloured or striped, jackets with the school coat of arms on, white shirts and ties with the school colours, obligatory for boys and girls alike, blue skirts, little caps and hats, glorious to behold. None of your sordid jeans and T shirts! That's what your pupils need here, English coats of many colours, to cheer up the scene!"

Gerald gazed into his glass of delicious Epesses. I could tell he was thinking.

"Yes, we in England possess a uniform culture," I went on, "even when you leave school you wear a special old school tie so everyone can recognize your class. And there are the club ties and striped jackets too, with badges, from rowing to bowing to the Queen. We have regimental ties to show you belonged to the best regiment and university uniforms by the score, academic dress for Doctors of Literature, Emeritus Professors of Darwin, in deep 3D colour, silk and gold adding to their genius. Each Cambridge college has its own colours, a veritable rainbow on procession day. How the world envies us our joyous sense of dress, Gerald! Then there are legal costumes too, our attorneys and lawyers and judges in gowns, wigs and furs according to rank. Chief Justices even have a 'working robe' for routine court work, just like our Lord Mayors of London who have no less than six different sets of robes including 'entertainment dress' used only when he is, yes, entertaining. Wonderful! And the taxpayers adore them too in their golden carriage, all sashes and orders and ribands in the wind! And his 'Aldermen' (selected local bufoons) and the Sheriffs and the Lords Lieutenant of the Counties of the Queen, in violet and blue, simply terrific! Then there are the Heralds from the College of Arms, stunning in mediaeval garb, who devise and supervise it all, a sort of Ministry of Costumes really, unique in the annals of human kind. And our House of Lords! Did you know a Duke is allowed a long robe with a 185 centimeter 'train' on the floor and a gold coronet with eight strawberry leaves, while his poor Duchess is only allowed a smaller crown with tiny leaves which has to be kept in place with a hair pin. Feminists please note. Never mind, ladies, look at the Queen in her sumptuous imperial shimmering robes of royal purple! Makes the world go green with envy, you know. Such outstanding uniforms are of course permitted only on certain days like the Queen's Birthday or the Restoration of Charles 1 by the reincarnation Society. This is all apart from the shiny uniforms of the Queen's personal order of Chivalry. We may have no sense of history, of course, Gerald, but, by God and all his miracles, our sense of pageantry is non pareil."

Then I had a stroke of genius.

"Gerald! Why not cheer up the whole population of Suisse Romande as well as just the pupils across the road?! Why not deck out the statues of Calvin, Knox and Zwingli in Geneva in some of our gorgeous English robes? The miniver, mink and ermine I feel would not only lead to a sartorial revival but to a religious one too!? People would worship again as they used to worship Queen Victoria in full regalia like her statue outside Buckingham Palace! What do you think?"

To my consternation, Gerald suddenly clutched his crotch and rushed out for the urinal.

Why is it that sometimes when I get some of my most inspired ideas, Gerald happens to choose just that moment to go for a piss?

"HIS HOBBY WAS HIS LIFE"

(inscription on an English tombstone)

I was watching the hords of Lac Leman boat enthusiasts from the sunny terrace of the Golden Sail overlooking the port. How these weekend sailors all cleaned and scrubbed and polished and varnished.

"Too much like hard work for me" I observed, " what we all need is a hobby which involves a lot of sitting down, we English are masters at this."

"Why?" queried my companion, Gerald de Vaud, raising his glass.

"Because we are a work avoidance society, Gerald. Cheers. We English work to finance our hobbies. What we do in the evenings and weekends is far more important than the mere money we earn during the week. In England, you wear your worst clothes for work and your best for your hobby. You make your biggest efforts for your part-time passion and your worst for your day to day job. An Englishman's hobby, you see, is his real career, that's why everyone thinks we're mad. Why an Englishman would regard it as a just inane if he thought he'd passed through this miraculous life only to leave full bank balances behind. A hobby, you see, is one's special contribution to life, one's distinction, one's individuality, unique and incomparable! And not just yachting or skiing on weekends like those conformist masses down there. Things far more subtle and lovely - from cabbages to kings."!"

"Pardon ?" asked Gerald, taking a sip of the lovely Villette.

"Like my own hobby!' I said, "Listen, Gerald, when I depart this world I intend to leave something memorable behind, not just silly lucre and a pathetic gold watch, something entirely mine, like, as it were," I savoured the next bit, "my superb collection of four hundred and forty nine Victorian toilet chains."

" What? Toilet chains?' Are you sure?"

"Of brass, of silver, even of gold, I assure you, many with royal connections! Oh, those wonderful ceramic handles with maker's name and symbol! When I see one of them, Gerald, I shiver with delight. But toilet chains are a modest endeavour, I assure you. I have a friend called Hope who collects angels. He has a collection of over one hundred and seventy of God's holy winged messengers to our world, in all materials from jesso to resounding bronze. All authenticated! He has them all in a monumental garden and they are the cynosure of all eyes. But there are less exalted hobbies too, like collecting dinosaur droppings (very popular since the film) or ferreting out Red Indian headdresses from the most unlikely of places. I have insurance friend has them on poles in his sitting room, and he wears only full Blackfoot costume, which he also collects, over the weekend and lives for that time in a wig-warn in his garden. He is respected all over town and never has trouble raising a bank loan. I know yet another who is a bus fanatic. I asked him on my last vacation, what number bus went to the station."

"6BUF 231," he replied.

"Priceless! I realized the number he gave me was not the route number of the bus but the registration number itself. Here was an Englishman who knew the registration numbers of the entire fleet of public buses! Pure genius! Not worth a penny of course but then that's the joy of it. Now that's what those weekend yachtsmen over there need: A touch of singularity in their lives. Imagine a Zurich bank director with his office hung with Victorian toilet chains! Or a Director of a School of Commerce giving classes on angel collecting! Or a Bernese Colonel of Alpine Infantry, turning out for military manoeuvres in Red Indian headress!"

Gerald was wide-eyed now.

"I need another drink after those delectable visions, "he said, "but, tell me, how do you get the time to cultivate all these first class hobbies of yours?"

"You take the time," I said, "with excuses, dental appointments, doctor's orders, often funerals. It all adds up, like time itself. The standard excuse is grandma. I have one friend who collects Irish beer-mats of the fifties and his grandma has died at least five times but he has the best beer-mat collection in the nation! Everyone knows, but at the same time everyone respects his life-enhancing passion, Irish beer mats, even his boss!"

"I don't exactly know why" said Gerald, "but sometimes you're very convincing!"
He suddenly fell clutching his side in agony.

"Are you all right Gerald?" I asked, very worried, for he was a good drinker.

"Suspected appendicitis, I'm afraid" he groaned, "tell them I won't be at school tomorrow. But, my friend, he added, getting to his feet, "entre nous, you will find me after school in my wine cellar - pursuing my favourite hobby!"

Dirt or The Golden Mean

My friend Gerald de Vaud and I were sitting at a cafe table opposite the Town Hall in the main Square, near the shores of Lake Geneva.

"It's far too clean here," I observed, "you could eat your brains off the cobbles.

What this place needs is some honest English dirt!"

Gerald looked thoughtful.

"You see Gerald, "I explained, "we English have a lifelong romance with absolute filth. We love the stuffs. Look at our public places, pavements covered with blackened blobs of chewing gum, paper wrappers, soiled tissues, empty packets of toiletries, super nappies, amazing condoms, marvellous bursting sacks of ordure in every road, pubs reeking with spilled beer, unswept trains, our garbage men leave even more garbage after they've called. They've elevated spreading dirt to a fine art! Bravo mes braves! One secret is, no bins; another is as few public toilets as possible. Works wonders. And with our medieval Saxon sort of plumbing, all our classes now share a delightful distaste for water, especially if it's in a bath. We affectionately call our lower classes, 'the Great Unwashed,' don't we? London's become one huge open air Mickey Mouse and Rat Race House.' Last year there were over 32,000 infestations of mice in the metropolitan area alone, and only 32 hygiene controllers to see them off! Bravo, London! Bravo British Mice! And bless our native rats too! 75% of our beaches are swimming in shit you can't even escape on the high seas. Wy, agesago, Cunard's luxury liner, a floating palace called Queen Elizabeth II, was once sued for having 'mouldy' lavatories, stinking corridors, bedrooms smelling of drains." "Splendid, of course" observed Gerald, "but don't you think this whole germ-loving thing has gone a bit far?"

"You're right, Gerald! Yes, England should be cleaned up a bit!

Moderation in all things, even moderation. But by the same token, this canton, and all the others too, should be dirtied up a bit as well. Imagine a few empty yellow crisp bags blowing over there in the spotless gutter, sticky coke cans rattling on the polished cobbles, piles of dried hooligan vomit in the immaculate shop doorways, with one or two London Waterloo beggars for local colour Eureka, I have it! Why not export our mountains of English filth? Garbage across the seas. Direct, out here! We lead the world in rubbish, don't we? - 'the dustbin of Europe.' I beg you, Gerald, leave it to Britain! Trust in our squalor. Our dirt is great and will humanize the earth."

"But don't look down on Swiss cleanliness, my friend."

"So practical! Where else to look? Go on!"

"A trade exchange perhaps?"

"Superb! I can see it! Yes! Battalions of Swiss cleaners in Picadilly Circus, cleaning up the debris of oafs and aristocrats, alongside your concierges, pest controllers, hygiene experts in Vaud costume all over Buckingham Palace binning the royal remains!"

"A vision straight out of paradise! I shall be there to see that, I promise you!" swore Gerald.

"Gerald, you realize what we're talking about, what mysterious force propels us on ?"

"What the old Greeks called, I believe, 'the Golden Mean.'"

"Spot on as ever," I applauded out loud, "the elemental shapes of perfection!"

We drank to our respective nations, united at last both in filth and hygiene and threw empty crisp packets to the winds to decorate the occasion and solemnize the pact. Cheers!

Embarrassment at Montreux

I was sitting in a cafe on the lake in the town of Montreux with my friend Gerald de Vaud when I noticed two workmen sitting at the bar a few tables away.

"Look, field labourers," I whispered, "the big one looks like a porker, and the small one like a fart. See their horny hands. I don't feel at ease with them so close. Why are they here anyway?"

" No snobs in our Canton," Gerald replied, "you can sit where you please."

"Listen, Gerald," I continued, "after all my travels I have concluded that the main problem in Europe and in Suisse Romande in particular, is that there is simply not enough class consciousness to go around. I am now convinced that a good dose of English snobbery would soon put people in their proper place, like those two workmen over there Look, wearing blue overalls just like workers in England."

"But why an English class system at all, my friend?"

"Because, Gerald, it would bring about world peace."

"Pardon?"

"Because, Gerald, everything in England is based on a system of calm transcendent snobbery. Everyone from erection to resurrection knows their place. "God bless the Squire and his relations and keep us in our proper stations" -- is our simple yet civilized outlook on life. That is why we have the most stable parliamentary democracy on earth. No one escapes. God bless our monarch and the snobbery she is Queen of! Gerald, I feel sure that if our caste system were introduced into Afghanistan, for example, it would bring about an instant cessation of hostilities. Who could resist it? The Basques too, the IRA. Why, even the mafia would fall adoringly at its feet instantly, giving up murder and dismemberment.

"How does this miracle of class work?" asked Gerald genuinely curious, as usual. "Well, like the Trinity, it goes in threes" I explained, "this café, for example, would be divided into three separate bars, with three separate entrances and three separate prices for the same beer. The public bar for the workers, the saloon bar for the middle classes and the private or lounge bar for the upper classes. Same for sport - football, darts or snooker for your 'proles' (prolateriat); rugby, tennis or yachting for your upper classes. Oxbridge for your aristocratical students, 'red-brick" (new) universities for your middle classes and cheerful 'Academies,' 'houses of correction' for your hooligan classes. *The Times* newspaper for your Tories, *The Telegraph* for your bank managers, and the *Daily Mirror* for your lower orders. Motorbike and dog races for your slaves, rowing for your masters. At Henly Rowing Regatta they just have a special 'Royal Enclosure' a sort of concentration camp for the creme de la creme, more difficult to get out of than old Adolf's gas chambers. And our rubbish too is so 'upper' and 'lower' that Harrod's recently introduced a 'sac a ordure' with their golden logo stamped on the side, a treasured item for your top nobs (cheap at ten francs a piece.) Even the humble potato is 'upper' or 'lower'. Your two grimy workers over there for example would call potatoes 'spuds' - awful, isn't it? Yes, I can tell an Englishman's class from a hundred metres in a fog. It's all a question of pose, poise, posture really."

I stood up then and did my elegant upper class poses, like the royals on the balcony of Buckingham Palace or our noble generals on their horse statues in the middle of Whitehall and other major thoroughfares. I even included the two workers in my princely gestures. I noticed they were now staring strangely at me. They got up, paid and began leaving. They paused at our table. "We're English, mate," the big porker said, slapping the palm of his hand with his fist, "doin' up the electrics for the jazz Festival, and we don't give a bugger what you say, everyone's entitled to their opinion, innit? But if you says one more word about our Queen, you'll end up double quick on the floor, with the laugh on the other side of you face, right, mate!?" They both smiled politely and made for the exit. Outraged, I rapidly ordered another bottle and we toasted old Albion and all her ways.

English Theme Parks Lead the World

My friend Gerald and I were sitting at a table in the Sports Park by the lake. Two sweating joggers toiled past.

"Do you jog?" asked Gerald.

"Only to the cellar" I replied, "Cheers!"

"So what do you think of our Sports Park by the lake, my friend?"

"Not enough poverty."

'Pardon?"

"It needs a few good old English 'Faginoramas'."

"What's a 'Fa-gin-orama'?"

"England's got thousands of them. Tourists love them."

"But what are they?"

"Theme Parks. A 'Faginorama' for example is a vision of Victorian squalor. Sort of Mary Poppins in reverse. Based on Charles Dickens a master of poverty and misery. Chimney pots, crooked rooves, dirty whores, filthy slums, dens of thieves, sweat shops, child labour, like Fagin's domain, get it?"

"Fag...fagin...faginorama', got it!"

"Terrific, yes? All fake of course, mostly plastic, even the tarts. We sometimes call these false pauper colonies of ours 'cardboard cities'. They look so real, lot of hard work there. You will observe them, Gerald, under our bridges, in our condemned buildings, deserted alleys, all over. Our Minister of Tourism recently moved bits of them into the Underground with musical instruments to cheer up the commuters - into shop doorways of the capital they go. Brilliant use of space! They imported real beggars from the Continent, surplus Romas and Latvians, to inhabit the (officially recognised!) sleeping bags provide for them in hedgerows and the discarded sofas of Luton town. Yes, the authentic touch works wonders! Why, we now supply Europe with over one quarter of its grinding poor! Super! But when you see this universal English beggary, Gerald, take no notice, it's all engineered, as I've just explained, to amuse the locals and divert the visitors "All the world' a stage" as the Bard of Avon wrote. So true. And after launching these metropolitan 'cardboard cities', the Minister of Illegal Immigrants established 'free enterprise zones' for more modern slum ghettos, soup kitchens, Salvation Army, sandwich centres, the Church's 'meals on wheels', missionary vicars and ministers all over the crypts - what a spectacle! Top hole Victorian nostagia trips for all the family. Bravo 'Faginorama', I say! Bravo Minister! Improves charity no end too. On top of this, our city open larceny programme's a tremendous success as well. Empire taught us there, universal pilfering, like in India and the Bahamas! More thefts in London now than in New York or Chicago. We lead the world in pillage! Here's a recent police list of the more original robberies: a High Court Judge's white horse-hair wigs, three children's paddling pools, with water, a complete 'heritage path' in the City, paving slabs recording England's greatness in verse, vanished! Two severed arms, complete with bandages and fingers, one police car, thirty-four dogs, including ten poodles and six Rotweilers - courage mes voleurs! Two earth removers, one complete hedge outside the Cuban Embassy and five bronze busts of Shakespeare - almost poetic, don't you think? And so official, all over the place, a huge success these sly snapper uppers, even the tourists join in! Soon have to nail down the grass, ha, ha! Now to share in our English genius for Theme Parks, I suggest over there by the luxury motor launches, a soup kitchen. Imagine! What dramatic contrast! And behind the vast yachting berths, a cardboard city all the way up to the Olympic Centre, to impress the athletes, especially those from the Third World. And on the superb new jetty there, clusters of filthy sleeping bags, all occupied of course, and around these splendid tables, assorted beggars of all ages and sexes, their hands outstretched, pleading in servile English accents and gestures, "Spare a penny, governor, sir, milord" with a tug of the forelock, the authentic touch again! All this as the Minister recently declared in the Commons, "to remind us that there is real poverty in the world and that in true Christian brotherhood we should always donate something, however little."

Gerald sat as one transfixed. To my astonishment, he looked a touch downcast. Then I understood! Like myself and our Ministries of Tourism everywhere, Gerald also had a troubled conscience about world poverty, and like me he was longing to donate, just donate, and to luxuriate in the fine feelings of accomplished charity. But the profound sadness when there's not one little beggar around to give a single centime to! But I would not let my friend down. I quickly walked over to the counter, took two one franc pieces out of my pocket, waved them to Gerald, and popped them in the St Bernardo's box with a most satisfactory 'clink!" Did he sit up? He did - laughing. "Bless our Faginoramas, I say!" I said, and shook the box, "What a receptacle for the goodness of the human heart! Cheers!"

Yes, I had made it clear to all and sundry that Gerald de Vaud, like all our English donators, had become just a little bit more of a man and a saint too.

Mr Marmalade

I was talking about jam with my friend Gerald de Vaud, at our stammtische, or usual places.

"You have wonderful jam" I observed "but something's gone badly wrong with ours1 It has developed a universal, virulent grey mold called 'Primus Mortalis"

"What in hell is that?" asked Gerald thoroughly alarmed.

"It comes under the Official Secrets Act but I tracked it down. Let me tell you about it."

"Of course," said Gerald, always curious to learn about our great royal island people.

"First clue to this deadly spoor I found, in of all places, the local library. It was under 'M' in the new Oxford dictionary. I asked the first class reference librarian there if he had any more on ' Primus mortalis' on the computer.

"Nothing," he told me, indicating an empty screen.

"But it's in the new Oxford Dictionary. Under 'cameronianesque,'" I insisted.

"Have you got any further facts about it?" he enquired.

"Of the basic causes, I am still ignorant but I do know some of the more deleterious effects. You see, some say Mr Cameron has no brains at all, just this cracked pot of mouldy English chunky marmalade thrust into his head in a botched operation. It's the sticky leaks from this pot that cause the worst infections apparently. Poor Cameron calls these leaks 'policies,' the foul things are dribbling all over the place, that's why the country's in such a mess."

The Librarian consulted his computer again,

“Yes! You’re right! Here it is, under ‘policies,’ he exclaimed,

“More of the symptoms, please.”

“...green shoots of despair, waste, incompetence... tons of those...”

“...anything more personal?”

“Etonitis, Oxbridge bonhomitis, Bullemitis, ‘no cure,’ it says. “Obsessive desire to spit on immigrants at the midnight hour and befoul the gutter press at dawn, and there’s a vicious tertiary strain, it says, a mold called ‘Charteritis’, which produces class delusions of well-being based on the promises of the Magna Charta, the Runnymede one, apparently. This paranoia has caused the most devastating depressions the slums have ever seen. But there are benign spoors here, too: love of warm Cotswold ale, invincible English suburban dogs, bright shadows of Thatcher and Churchill on summer eves, loyal English cricket grounds and other shining examples. ...”

“Enough!” I said, “to the core of the potted carbuncle now and its detestable leakages!

What’s new?”

“The ailments of the great...” the librarian read out again, “look, Roosevelt, Kennedy, Nixon, Ivan the Terrible. They all suffered from the scourge of chunky marmalade with its great orange leaks, it nearly finished them off.”

“What saved the English in particular ?” asked Gerald.

“Not charteritis, not Bullititis or any other ‘itis,’ just practical English common sense,” said the librarian overcome with British patriotism, even his accent became a bit public school, “posh dissidents, all Tories, of course, who were passed over for a job, hired an immigrant assassin who secured entry to Chequers, bashed the PM imbecile over the head, opened it, subtracted all the malign juices in one scoop, substituted the milk of human kindness and then let it all curdle there, so it became as bland and as slowly absolutely yuk as every policy had been before! They extracted the smelly old PM at the next general election, ossified in marmalade juice, another prominent victim of 'primus mortalis'!

"What a fall was there from his first major appointment as Parliamentary Consultant to the Guild of British Glass Makers!" shouted the librarian, now waving a paper union jack.

"What an epitaph goes there!" I couldn't help adding.

"And, look, I've tracked it down! Here is its generic name! - "Statitis Quoitis!"

"Well spoken!" exclaimed Gerald, "problem solved, tho' it is a mouthful."

"So, Gerald, a plague on all their houses! Let's celebrate the solution of the Mystery of the Chunky Marmalade!"

And so we did, with a priceless Epesses '92.

Don't Hurry, drink Calamin

I was sitting at a table on a sunlit terrace in Grand Vaud overlooking sparkling Lake Leman enjoying a superbly modest Calamin. I pointed at the serried terraces below.

"Vines are calm" I observed to my friend Gerald de Vaud, "yet they work as hard as we. But look," I indicated a group of workmen re-laying the road as if it was leading to the Gold Rush, and at the waiters running around like they were Stock Exchange jobbers, "Behold their sweated brows. And see the results. It's simply not worth it!"

I sipped again. The Cálamin refreshed my whole being, "Englishmen are like vines too," I observed, wise in my cups, "they never hurry, they achieve maturity at just the right time and are rarely blown away. All due to our 'stiff upper lip', our phlegm. Like plants, we never panic. If for example you were seen in England running like those waiters and labourers there, you d be asked at once even by casual passers by, "Where's the fire?" Secret is, never hurry to work, only hurry from it. And never sound your horn. A simple London bus driver once showed the world. I watched him, public transport held up by a lady loading her car with silly shopping. A huge long jam. Did he yell? Did he sound his horn? No! He rested his foot on the brakes and read his newspaper! Which reminds me, I once bought a shirt, no hurry. The assistant pointed to his ladder, looked at me and said "Help yourself, mate, you climb up, I'm listening to the cricket news." No panic. No rat race. No promotion. Why, your roads in the towns here in Switzerland look like third-rate racing circuits run by bad- tempered amateurs, going - where? Whereas we English are masters of nonchalance, princes of insouciance. And remember we won! We won at Agincourt, we won at Waterloo, we won in '45. The Nazi Wehrmacht SS couldn't believe it! We won because we didn't rush! Stiff upper lip! Have you ever seen an Englishman escorted to his execution? He strolls! And didn't Charles II apologise for "taking an unconscionable time a'dying." What a stroller there! Yes, 'stroll' is the favourite word of all Englishmen, and heedlessness his view of the world. Then I had an inspiration. Again! I moved in with deliberation, "You should establish Cantonal centres of Nonchalance here, Gerald, Schools of Strolling in Vaud, Academies of Cool, you've got enough wine. Then you could watch the Vaudois stroll to work at eight like slugs. Forget to be at work at eight. Be late. Forget being late! Take the day off! - go to your grandmother's fourth funeral, do your hobby, swing from your favourite hammock. Stroll, stroll, stroll, in mid air if need be! I can see it! The gnomes of Zurich playing slow bowls, responsible teachers sipping Calamin in class, banker fishing in the dark, students screwing in daylight! All on Monday! Suisse Romande full of massed graduates of Cool, Doctors of Nochalance, Strollers cum laude, Uni Profs of TIE, Take it Easy! And with Calamin on their side, they'd win every time! And you Vaudois would end up like us, in a bloody great mess but having universal fun, no panic in the toilets, and no glum chums!"

"Why then...?" asked Gerald looking cooly at me, "why are you in such a hurry when you're drinking, you're on your third bottle already!?"

"Well, I do admit, Gerald, that's the one thing I do enjoy hurrying about. In fact I'd love to arrive first. Cheers!"

"Cheers!" said Gerald and we drank - so cool, so English, so... Calamin! And we both arrived first!

Eccentric is OK in the UK

Gerald and I were sipping an ale named after one of England's finest poets, Thomas Hardy.

"It has a nutty, rounded, fabulous after-taste." remarked Gerald, smacking his lips and re-filling his glass.

"Not often you find a beer named after a poet," I observed, "but in England eccentric is OK. In fact it's normal. Take the Marquis of Bath. He sports a pony-tail and has half a dozen mistresses whom he calls 'wifelettes' in his barns. His father introduced lions onto the family estate.' Some are still there. When the Marquis enters the House of Lords, no one raises an eyebrow. And listen, down the road from my house, a man stuck a 'huge plastic dolphin into his roof, so it looked like it had just dived out of the skies. And what happened? The whole neighbourhood applauded. Which reminds me of the Reverend Valentine Fletcher, he collected chimney pots and displayed them in his front garden - a veritable forest of chimney pots, over two hundred in fact. And the fate of the smokeless divine? Why he was loved even more by his parishioners. Or another friend of mine who wears polo mints as cuff-links. And yet another who in his quest for anonymity used to go to the cinema and hide under an open umbrella so no one would notice him. And *why* not? Live and let live. Another acquaintance of mine gave up his job to widen his search for 'namealikes'. He's found William Shakespeare who's a plumber in Windsor, Michael Jackson who's a bus driver in Rhyl, Paul Newman, a retired ironmonger who lives in Bedford down by the river, a delightful spot. My friend's got hundreds of such 'name-alikes'. And the result? Why, whenever he meets any of his old work mates, they always want to by him drinks and hear of his new amazing nomenclatures. They respect him far more than their boss. He' is a very fullifilled person.Then take our late beloved once Poet Laureate, John Betjeman. He saved a railway station with his verse. He wrote a poem on the beauty of Ditton Marsh Halt which was slated for closure, but the travelers recited the poems in unison to the government and Ditton Marsh was reprieved. Same with a closed Welsh pub, the local poet wrote a poem on the shutters lamenting the loss of such a fine watering hole. A retired couple read the poem and loved it so much they bought and re-opened the pub. Not often you get poets saving pubs and stations but in the UK it's OK. And didn't another song writer, Noel Coward who lived deep in fine wine territory above Montreux write, 'Mad dogs and Englishmen go out in the midday sun"? He was right. Another English neighbour of mine got very famous last year by owning the Champion Talking Parrot of 2012. Everybody really envied him for that, a life- enhancing achievement.

To trains again. Why, last week I heard this announcement, "The train now standing at Platform Three will take off in five minutes!" And, "We apologise for the delay of the 9.45. This was due to a complete cockup!" And lastly, "Will the children now on holiday remember to give the grown ups a happy day as welL" Everybody was delighted. And last Saturday they stopped a train during lunch hour and carried out a search for a boa-constrictor. Everyone joined in. It turned out to be just a joke. No one complained. Indeed, they just laughed and put it down to a relaxed way of life.

Even cats can take part in this eccentric jamboree. Reg, who is Welsh, is known as the Carmarthen 'boomerang' cat because he always comes back. When he sees an open door, cars, trains, charabancs, he always jumps aboard - but he always returns - hence 'boomerang.' I'd like to see more cats like that here in this very canton, more unorthodox parrots, more 'wifelettes' in the barns of Vaud, more polo mint cuff-links for bank directors, stations more open to verses, more travelers who recite poetry on chimney pots, more announcers who say "cock up!" That sort of thing. And why not appoint a Vaudois poet as champion? Make him really revered, then you can applaud him every Sunday, like my own Vicar Valentine. I really fail to see any objection to this. Didn't the renowned philosopher George Santayana once remark, "England is the paradise of eccentricity, heresy, anomolies, hobbies and humours." He's right of course, but we call it normal. These daily delights of ours don't cost a centime and they help us to be civilized. That great quality could be yours too!" I paused. "Gerald!" I chided abruptly - I hadn't noticed so taken was I with our little chat - "may I say that it's not very civilized to have finished our Thomas Hardy ale in one swig. And I'm as thirsty as any Vaudois, I assure you!"

"I was just being eccentric" replied Gerald with a broad smile, "I'm happy. And I intend to be so again when you order the next bottle of Thomas Hardy ale for us both! Cheers!"

Great Players

We were sitting in the Black Cat, the famous before and after theatre cafe in the centre of the little Swiss town. We had just been to see the local English Group of players perform *Funny Face, a* Hollywood comedy.

"Marvelous," said Gerald, "and the actors were all just business men, teachers, secretaries – amateurs, you said."

"Amateurs!" I repeated, "you have just paid them the greatest compliment. We are the finest actors in the world and it's all based on the cult of the amateur."

I explained on, "Wherever we go, we do two things, build Empires and act in them. There isn't an Englishman, on earth who hasn't acted. Even as skinny prisoners of war of the Japanese, we dressed up in ballet skirts and acted. Our royals act, Princes Charles and Edward. Wasn't one of our Prime Minister's Dad a trapeze artist! English actors are made into Lords, Knights and millionaires, Sir Anthony Hopkins, Lord Olivier, Sir Michael Caine. We win Oscar after Oscar, palmes d'or galore. Our costume drama sweeps the world! Yes, pageants, pantomimes, theme parks, parades, costumes, the Lord Mayor's annual procession, coronations, enoblements, investitures, as well as school, amateur and professional plays, pantomimes, masked balls and fancy dress parties, all part of the picture, delightful productions every one! "

"Look at me," said Gerald, "a Swiss who knows his Shakespeare but who's never been near a stage. But how is it so widespread in England?"

"Starts at school, my friend. Every school in the UK has a small theatre and a 'Speech Day' and the high point of this is the 'School play', any play from Hamlet to Jesus Christ Superstar, with half the school on stage. This is how the Beatles and Rolling Stones were veteran performers at fifteen. The Royal Shakespeare Company and the

National Theatre are controlled by ex-Oxbridge students, with no professional qualifications at all - inspired amateurs. And after the horrible choice of a career, more thespian fun! In the UK there are thousands upon thousands of amateur groups, nobody knows how many. Every village has a theatre group and a village hall with a stage. There are hundreds of annual amateur play festivals, competitions, trophies, conferences, summer schools with a thousand courses on make-up, costume, special effects including wind and snow machines, lots with local bank sponsorship. During last September and October alone there were over eight hundred amateur first nights. Many famous actors have started out in these small village theatres. And it's all so well run. The theatre is about the only thing in England that starts on time. Why, the Windmill Theatre never missed a performance during the entire blitz and opened on time even when Nazi bombs were raining down. If we paid the same attention to our economy, we'd be the richest country on the planet. "Why do all Englishmen act?" you ask, Gerald? Well, I believe, because of his 'stiff upper lip', his traditional phlegm, sangfroid. He can't emote in private but by God he can do it on stage where he's safe! Only an Englishman saves up his real feelings for a place of illusion. Paradoxical, but it's only there he can bare his heart. He's at his most alive in a mask. And why? Because it is only on stage he can transcend the class he's born into. In a play, he's achieved a state of classlessness at last. Nirvana to the general! Now the local butcher can be the aristocrat and the aristocrat the local butcher. The great escape! Half a nation in search of a character! What a relief! What explosions of emotion! All there on stage, incarnate! The furiosus Saxonus catharsis with Oscars on top! Show me an Englishman on stage and I'll show the happiest man in the world!"

"After seeing *Funny Face* " Gerald said enthusiastically, " I can only agree. Cheers!"

An Uneasy Meal

One warm June evening I met my friend, Gerald de Vaud at our table of a restaurant by the lakeside. I was surprised that he hadn't asked me to join him but knew exactly why when I saw what he was eating. The dish gave me the first uneasy meal I had ever had with my dear friend. A whole pile of minute bones were rising obscenely on his plate.

"Gerald" I asked, "how can you eat frog's legs?"

He washed his fingers and poured me a generous glass of 'Johannis' - rather a sweet wine but sufficient unto the day - and motioned for me to sit.

"We call the French 'froggies' because of what you're doing," I pressed on, "you must be on your fiftieth poor frog already."

"I like frogs' legs," drooled Gerald, licking a tiny thigh bone just to provoke me, "and snails and brains..."

"Please, Gerald" I begged, "I'm trying to eat this roll too!"

" And ostrich legs and horse stakes!"

"Cruelty to animals!" I hushed him, "I shall contact Animal Rights."

"But you admitted yourself yesterday the English didn't know anything about food. What about that infamous British sandwich you told me about?"

I saw a way to take my revenge.

"The luscious English 'butty' sandwich, you mean, where you fill two slices of soggy white bread with margarine, then add thick greasy chips?"

'Please," pleaded Gerald, "I'm eating too. You're a nation surrounded by sea," he counter attacked,

"and you have to go to Paris for a decent fish dish. And didn't someone of your acquaintance recently ask for 'brown sauce on her lobster thermidor?'

"Well, eating with your fingers isn't very polite either."

"You said yesterday the English ate like hogs."

"I meant the lower orders, the hooligans."

"Like that lady you took out to dinner in the village on Friday?"

"She was of noble birth and entitled to a few eccentricities."

"Like blowing her nose on the napkin?"

"She had a cold, poor thing."

"And taking her budgerigar to your table."

"It was lonely."

"And complaining her hors d'ouevres were the same colour as the dessert ...'

"...she is very artistic,.."

"..and the 'sheep were too loud, the cows 'of an objectionable hue,' the ducks too agressive..."

"...you disapproved of all this too,' he insisted.

"I admit frankly" I said warmly, I wanted to be friends again, "that I did say it was outrageous that we English were still charged for the froth on our beer. Why, sixty four per cent of all our pints are four per cent short of beer. This is against the Magna Carta of 1215, the first Bill of Civil Liberties signed and in England!"

"Salut to the Magna Carta then!" said Gerald with great sincerity.

"Just remember one thing, please, she was upper class, that's all.

"So it was OK for her to ask the maitre d' 'to doggie bag' the rest of her canard a 1' orange?"

"She hates waste."

"For 'her goats?"

"She loves animals."

"I hope the maitre d' did! ' And she treated the waiters like peasants'," I am quoting you again, my friend.

"But they were peasants."

"So she was entitled not to say 'please' or 'thank you?"

"The waiters were saying that enough for us all," I said soothingly, "remember, as I said, she is of ancient lineage."

"Ancient bad manners too."

"She is a Marchioness. There, I have told you!"

"So bad manners only become 'obscenities' when employed by 'the lower orders'?"

"Exactly, Gerald, you understand at last."

Gerald looked astonished and seemed to withdraw any further objections.

"And of course I do admit as I said yesterday that some things in English cuisine do appear to elude the normal urge for culinary perfection. Didn't I give you a mock English menu: three-year old salmon, never mind salmonella, six- year old frozen Spanish beef, never mind the 'mad cow disease...'

"...which no other nation would touch...

"...disgraceful I agree! - one-day old wine, four-year old coffee, two million year old salt, and one-hundred million year old mineral water from the glaciers of the pre-Jurassic age in Scotland! We do not legally have to declare age in England, you see, and it's a scandal as I most vehemently admitted, yes?"

Gerald seemed reconciled.

“Now to show my deep regard for you, for when you next eat in London, an inside tip so you are not embarrassed. Black Forest gateau is out. Bread and butter pudding is in!”

“Thank you” said Gerald gravely, “ ‘bread and butter pudding’ “ I shall pass that on to the Head waiter at once.”

I smiled with relief.

“Go on” I said, “I don’t mind, have more frogs’ legs if you wish.”

“Fine,” laughed Gerald, ‘but only if you have a ‘butty’ sandwich!”

And thus we parted, our appetites satisfied, the best of friends again.

Tory Rule or the 'Old Boy Net'

We had just met up in London and my pal Gerald and I were having a drink in the Strand. "But the homeless?" said Gerald, puzzled, "there are beggars in every doorway. England must be poor." We were chatting in The Duke of Wellington near Fleet Street. Gerald was staying for a long weekend. He was on the hunt for the famous English Burberry overcoat.

"No, Gerald" I explained, "the wealth of the country has simply been sequestered. It is in the right hands, never fear."

"And who are these 'right people'?"

"Tory rulers in the 'old boy net."

"What is this 'net'?"

"Net' is network 'old boy' is an old public school chum or former colleague. To be in this fabulous net, as I am, you must go to exclusive private schools from the age of six to eighteen. Theft you must go to an exclusive university, Oxford or Cambridge, known as 'Oxbridge.' There are thirty-one top private schools todayJ The Clarendon Report of 1861 noted thirty. In this century only Ampleforth has joined the magic circle. A wonderful stationary pyramid of influence and privilege has been built up over one hundred and thirty years and is still intact, you see, because it is self perpetuating. Eton in Windsor, for example is still number one. It has produced more prime ministers than any other school. It is said that the battle of Waterloo was won on the playing fields of Eton. So if you're an old Etonian and you go to Cambridge, Trinity College, where Prince Charles studied, then you're in the old boy net. Sometimes, upper class embryos are put down for Eton on conception."

Gerald gulped on his Guiness.

"But how do you know who went to which school?" he asked in

curiously strangled tones.

"Old school ties, also by stance, pose, more than anything else, by accent."

"Accent?"

"More of that later, Gerald. After Oxbridge, you go into the Diplomatic Corps, or the Foreign Office - the present Cabinet are old Etonians - the Judiciary, the Civil Service, the army, and top family banks in the City if you want to go into. Very few of the top bankers have any commercial qualifications at all, Oxbridge does the trick. At the moment the six senior UK ambassadors are all Oxbridge and private school. Mr Cameron's new "one society" was so effective that sixteen ministers out of twenty in his first Cabinet, were Oxbridge. All went to elite private schools, of course."

"But do these private schools provide a good education?"

"That's not the point Gerald,' I explained patiently, "you go there for contacts, not for education, that's why we have such imbeciles at the top. In England we have institutionalized ignorance. The rest is pretence, Napoleon's famous 'Albion perfide.'"

"But" said Gerald" concentrating on his pint of Guiness, he had recently fallen in love with this Irish elixir.

"Isn't that all a bit unfair."

"Not at all, my friend. The Tory principle is simple, 'the country is best left to those who own most of it, for they will fight hardest because they have the most to lose.' And that has worked so well over the last 500 years that 90% of the land here, for example is now owned by 13% of the population. Out of 125 senior judges, 105 are Oxbridge. Just right. There are only three women there, thank God! At the moment the offices of Home Secretary, the Ministries of Defense, Social Services, Environment, Defence, to name but a few are not only run by Oxbridge men but by contemporary Oxbridge chums. Wonderful bonding, miraculous unity. Out of about 308 Tory Mp's, over 200 went to private schools. Not one Tory MP has noted in his CV the dreaded words, "manual labourer" like carpenter or seaman. Not one. A pure breed of Platonic Guardians, Victorian Knights in shining armour, every one! And how'd you fit all this perfection into the Social Charter of the EU? You can't! Those frogs over there are mad! Mr Cameron is right, don't meddle with the wonderful social basics of our society."

"But didn't Chancellor Helmut Schmidt once say that as long as you maintained that "damned class-ridden society of yours, you'd never get out of your mess! ?"

"Silly fellow! Our Old Boy Net is as immovable as the Great Pyramid!"

"But the mass of the people, the beggars and homeless out there, how do you keep them down?"

"Simple, by state education, they keep themselves down after that, I assure you, then when adult, rule them by quangoes."

"What are these 'Quangos'?"

"More of those later. Firstly, in the European community in both Education and Training, the UK comes 22nd out of 22. And this is no accident. In state schools only 14% get their baccalauriat. In elite private schools, *65%.* In Germany 63% of German workers have technical qualifications. Here, only 23%. Simple, the Education Minister is Oxbridge, so you just cut back on the education budget. The rest of the donkeys are amenable enough, though I do think we've gone into over-production with hooligans. No empire to write them off in, you see."

'Pity about that," said Gerald, "otherwise you could send all the beggars and the homeless out there to die for their country." "Exactly, my friend. You grasp the point admirably. Wait till you've bought that Burberry coat, that's an Oxbridge symbol too. You get automatic respect."

"I don't think I'll be getting a Burberry after all. Shop around a bit." Had I said anything wrong?

"But why, Gerald?" I asked worriedly.

"Because I think I'll spend the money on Guiness instead!" What a joker! What a friend!

Gerald de Vaud is one foreigner who's got his priorities right!

The Magic of Quangos

I was again sitting over a half bottle of the vastly improved Morges wine in the Cafe Romande, centre of Cantonal genius, culture and civilized debate.

"Yes," I said to my friend, Gerald, expert in the ubiquitous English 'gerund, "the Tory quango is a wondrous beast!"

"But what does 'quango' mean?" asked Gerald.

Such an inquiring mind, such a sympathetic ear! I do believe he'll be taking out English nationality next!

"Literally, 'quango' means 'quasi autonomous national government orgamzation.'"

"I'm sorry, I'm still lost."

"Never mind, so is the whole of Europe, especially Brussels! Let me explain. We Tories have now been in power for years and years, right? And we are leaving the indelible mark of our own superior form of government on Europe as well as in Merrie England, OK?"

"Yes, but what form do these superiorities take – are they animal, vegetable or mineral?"

What a sense of humour! But it concealed a serious question.

"Perhaps I could best illustrate my answer by referring to my favourite colony, Wales. Now Wales is governed by its own Assembly which says it can never be independent. So, by usage and education, not to mention quangoes, the people call for a pint whenever they hear the word 'politics', and vote for the old guard, all on the old boy net principle, but on the left. Perfide Albion again! Now, this is the point, 'quangos' make up this ' Administration,' like power used to be centralised in 'departments' in Whitehall, London, in the magnificent former days of empire! And nothing of the old values are lost."

Gerald nodded sagely. He is one of the few foreigners I know whose respect for the peculiarities of English rule is consistent and unmistakable - if a little off-beat , even 'federation' at times.

"Now to the core," I pressed on, "In the absence of a better word, a 'quango' therefore is a committee friendly only to the Tory party. They are, not to put too fine a point on it, centres of patronage for leaders of privilege. You set up a 'quango' when, frankly again, you want to carve up a particular sector and share the spoils with your pals in the old boy net. So, the Assembly Member of Wales, seizes upon, say, a hospital which he has personally decided to 'privatise.' He next sets up a 'quango' over it, dominated by his Tory pals, all on inflated fees. In Wales you have quangos on Education, Hospitals, Colleges, Schools, Broadcasting, Tourism, Gas, Marine Development, Coal, etcetera, a total of about eighty. You even have chaps called 'Kings of the Quango', old boys who hold multiple quango appointments, in much the same way as you can have as many as six 'quangos' over a single school, why not? Whatever the public outcry that one time, there was enough cash to go round!" I had the bit between my teeth now, "The the First Minister and his quangoes control a budget of 2,1 billion pounds single-handed and can offer his friends a choice of over 1,400 appointments - no interview or CV required - and no ability either! Yes, in our Tory paradise there are always rich pickings! And the biggest quango of all is of course at the moment, Herr Cameron's Public School marmalade Cabinet. You see, to use a Shakespearean image, a 'quango,' and our unique class system too, is like a beautiful big onion, there is always another layer! That is part of the essential magic of our genius. But there is also another marvelous ingredient, anonymity. 'Quangos' are faceless. Makes you chuckle, doesn't it?! You don't have to publically announce a quango. You don't have to disclose whom you appoint. None of the members are known locally. No one knows where the quango 'deliberates.' There is no public scrutiny, no accountability. All is a total blank! You wake up one morning, and bingo! like an overnight mushroom (to pursue the Shakespeare vegetable image!) the quango, like Mount Everest, is just there! Well, from my, notes, let me conclude. The same system reigns throughout the UK. The regions of England, thank God, have now reverted, like Wales, to domestic colonial status and are treated as such. In fact, so much so that the recent 329.24 million pounds granted for 'regional development' by the European Parliament, will in England be chanelled into, yes! our sly 'quangos' and our Oxbridge universities! Does that answer your question, Gerald?" I asked, looking up.

To my astonishment Gerald had disappeared, as is his wont sometimes. This time I found him in the toilet clutching his stomach.

"I just puked," he gasped."Something you ate, my friend?"

"Something indigestable all right," he muttered.

"Well come and sit down again, "I urged "and have a nice cup of tea, that will settle your stomach, I still want you to tell me about all these dreadful referendums you have to put up with in the Canton of Vaud."

Unfortunately, Gerald was again seized by nausea. However I was glad to see that he quickly got better in the fresh air outside. And as we walked to the next cafe, I had a feeling the magic influence of English 'quangos' had helped him to recover!

The European Union - England's Adultery

I was sitting in a replica English pub close to Lake Leman. Although the place was fake, it brought at least a whiff of civilization. I was waiting for my friend Gerald de Vaud. We were going on an ale-tasting trip around town.

At the next table were a group of embittered English expats, typical of the recent type of Brit traitors and national adulterers. How they moaned! Off and on about the Social Chapter of the EU and how we should 'opt out.'

"So the Conservatives saved the British sausage," I heard one of them braying. Such trash! What frivolity! But I was determined not to be drawn.

"Article 118a of the Social Chapter is ruinous to the British way of life," I thought to myself.

"What crazy demands it makes: consultative bodies for workers, freedom of information, open recruitment, fair play for part-timers, all for the workers. Ugh! And why 'protect' children from seven to fifteen? They mature so rapidly these days.

"No!" I nearly said out loud, "Away with all wages councils, unfair dismissal legislation and a statutory minimum wage! They just don't fit in with the right people! We alone know how to deal with our own serfs, çoolies, felaheen, hooligans, kids, untouchables and our teeming 'undeserving poor.' Our sovereignty! Our option! Our Minister put it so rightly, 'We want policies made in Britain, for Britain and by the British Parliament!' The twenty-two countries of Europe do not fit into our class system and they don't even know it. Even the House of Lords is a mystery to them! So we're snobs, you say? So what! Our choice! And who hasn't got 'lower orders' in their own countries? We true blue Tories are battling for absolute inequality. Again, our choice! And demented froggies and Huns say the Brits want "a return to the days of sending children up chimneys.' You bet we do! Our choice again! We advertise Britain as a 'low wage' country. That's the huge advantage the 'opt out' gives us. And who were once 'low earners'? Why, the Japs and the Koreans, the business success stories of the world. Yes, we have never been better armed for the future. It is us who is changing the face of Europe! And those typical foreign continentals who come over here and exploit our over-generous social security sevices! The Minister described them aptly, "Mama Mias's on a 'crook's tour of England!" Brilliant!

Every Tory recognizes the indisputable fact that a foreign accent is a public confession of criminal intent. Damn those betrayers! So noisy! "Yes," I thought, "we have a prison population of over 77, 000. Not enough! More at the next table! A pleasing memory struck me then, the promise of 'floating prisons', due to overcrowding. Bring back the hulks! - just right for those traitors. I listened. More frivolity about "the workers" again. I had to do something. I got three beer mats and wrote a telling quotation on each, "The outlook of the Community is quintessentailly un-English!" - Mrs Thatcher.' And, "The Social Chapter is directly against everything in which we believe," the Cabinet Minister. And thirdly, "Back to basic British values of neighbourliness, decency and courtesy!"

"Cheers, mate!" I heard one of them say. "Mate!"?I gritted my teeth.

"Yes," I thought, "those continentals have just spent 8,140 million pounds on the European Parliament building in Brussels."

I amused myself by making computations on what the money might have been spent on - one bottle of champagne for every adult in Britain! Or a new bike, or a trip for seven million kids to Disneyland, a pint of good British beer for every inhabitant of Europe. And a wicked thrust now, a grey suit for every adult in Belgium. And naughty - a one-way trip to Brussels for every Afghanistani warrior!

"Yes," I heard one of the ex-pats declare bombastically, "Those Tory Little Englanders, elitist school bullies! Down with their elective tyranny, down with their parliamentary absolutism!" What gibberish!

"Prisons, patriotism and secrecy' that's their creed!"

"What lying bilge" I said out loud. I couldn't help it.

"I nearly reminded them that our present pro-European Foreign Secretary is being accused of expenses fraud under the Treason Act of 1795, the Act of Settlement of 1700 and the Coronation Oath Act of 1953! A traitor! The days of such Quislings are numbered! Bloody British justice is bloody blind!" they just gaped.Hell, I had to do something. I passed over the beer mats.

This only caused hoots of coarse, vulgar laughter.

"You're right," one hooligan exclaimed sarcastically at me, "those foreigners, all they want is to rape our gracious Queen!"

That did it! I dragged the swine to his feet. I drew back my fist. They could scarcely believe it. Then a hand suddenly seized my wrist and held me back. It was Gerald.

"Don't" he said soothingly, "they're not worth it."

"Exactly what we were saying about this nasty, loony little sod," said the one of the creeps.

Gerald had to drag me away. I have always been prepared to give my life for the honour of my country and to punch a lower class twerp has always been one of my ambitions.

"Thank God you don't have such traitors and adulterers in the Canton de Vaud!" I said to Gerald. But even Gerald seemed strangely distant for the rest of the evening.

The English Gentleman and his Club

"The one thing you lack in this Canton of Vaud, 'as I have observed before, Gerald, are a few real nobles, a Duke de Montreux, a Vicomte de Villette, a Marquis of Zurich."

Gerald laughed so hard I thought he'd split.

We were sitting at a cafe by the lake. Directly to the left of us was a statute of Major Davel, would be Liberator of Vaud. "All very well having a Liberator" I thought "but you need a few gentlemen as well."

"Even a few younger sons of the nobility would do out here," I said, "those with only 'Honourable' before their name, seeing that in England the eldest son inherits all."

"The entire title?" said Gerald, holding his sides. He seemed to find the entire subject hilarious. I decided to humour, if not entertain him. After all his quaint peasant customs had often caused me a hidden smile.

"You could establish gentlemen's clubs here, honestly. In England there are 127 ranks above 'gentleman' and 109 before the wives of gentlemen. We have 25 dukes, 37 Marquises, 110 Viscountancies, 173 earls, 438 Barons. Over seven thousand citizens can in fact claim a title. Nothing wrong with a touch of Lordolatry. We have only about forty exclusive clubs in all. But having so few nobles in Vaud, you'd only need one or two. Don't forget to situate the clubs near the seats of power, because that's basically what they're all about. Ours are near Parliament Square and the royal palaces. The aristocracy favours the area around St James, the more parvenu politicians, millionaires and vulgar mechanics, like the discoverers of penicillin or the splitters of atoms, choose Pall Mall, such as the Athenium. You only get elected by other members, so new members are always 'the right type', say Eton and Oxbridge. On the walls inside are the coats of arms of the private schools and universities the clubs are most closely associated with, Harrow, King's etc. More gentleman bonding, superb! Remember above all, Gerald, "to thine own self be true," "never a swot, a swank or slacker be."

And you should hear some of their amazing names. Listen, "Leone Sextus, Denys Oswolf, Fraduati Tollemache, Tollemache-de Orellano-Plantagenet Tollemach-Tollemache," a simple major killed in the First Word War. My favourite! I like " Captain Sir Reginald Aylmer Ranfurly Plunkett Ernle Erlea Drax" too.

Gerald was rolling on the ground with mirth, breathless. Such a character!

"Do get up, Gerald" I begged, "there's more to come. Yes, you should see some of these piles! Like Renaissance Palazzi or Greek Acropolises, marvellous! By-words in luxury and elegance, town retreats for our upper class urban princes, the invisible elite of the nation. They alone possess the inbred right to total inequality and to hold up themselves as post-colonial knights, the incarnation of the best in European humanism! But the top clubs are very exemplars of discretion too. There is no name plate at the entrance. There is no address on your visiting card or in your entry in *Who's Who,* just *White's'* or *'Brook's'.* Like our national stamps, there's no 'England' or GB on them, just the Queen's profile, that's enough for the world. And no one knows how rich they are, like the Church or the Queen or closed corporations like Oxford and Cambridge. 'Secrecy' the vulgar call it. I call it 'natural selection.' Anyone who is anyone knows instinctively where to look, that's my point. In the blood, as it were. If you say *'White's'* to a taxi dryer, he'll tug his forelock and you'll be there in five minutes. Yes, you may laugh, but our servants are as deferential now as they were under Prince von Rupert of Hanover.
Yes, the name of your club is the password to the highest circles in the land. I now decided on a few of my famous regal imitations, poses and stances. People around looked up and began laughing. I played up to

them. I strutted like a Prince, smiled a 'noblesse oblige' smile. They all shouted encouragement.

"Now the aristocracy is noted for its 'stiff upper lip" I said so the whole terrace could hear,

"and more especially, by that wonderful English trait, 'understatement.' Understatement is calling your castle a 'damp summer house', your vast estates, 'sort of ruined gardens' or World War II, 'a bit of a party down the road.' The Duke of Westminster who owns half of central London once confessed that his three billion fortune represented "quite sufficient earnings." Your top 'aristo' will also eschew vulgar display. His perfectly cut tweeds will be slightly worn, his car 'an old banger' needing repair, his furnishings at home frayed and faded - visual understatements, as it were. Moreover, to add still more charm, there are the noted aristocratic affectations, a calculated stammer, a practised lisp, a superb listlessness and a seeming endless *vacuity* of mind.

"Awistocwats' a Viscount might say, "are just ord... ordin... ordinaw... cha.. cha... cha... chappies aftah awl." And why this eccentric overlay? To mask their cunning and their wealth! And to maintain it against all comers! These Scarlet Pimpernels slither in the undergrowth of Anglo power like snakes! And they're deadly too. Remember 007 was Eton and *Blade's* and he was licensed to kill! They will tear your balls off to maintain their privileges. You try and steal one pheasant from their estates and you're for the scaffold. Our present Home Secretary is currently smashing the anti-Fox Hunting league. What rotters! And why not? These hippy types are not part of the traditional upper class English countryside. Who are the clubs' most deadly enemy then? The Prolateriat? Never! They exist in another world, Disraeli's *Two Nations*. Your workers are too far gone in subservience anyway. No, the true enemy of the English gentleman are the socially ambitious middle classes. 'Gentility' and the upper class 'gentleman' was invented for the very purpose of keeping the middle classes in their proper place. You can always tell by their excruciating imitation upper class accents. And the system works! Just go into one of these miraculous centres of excellence, *White's* or *Brook's,* and you will fall in love with the English gentleman and his club. And you will never want to change it, the exact aim of the Higher Ones!

"A real 'gentleman' as one 'aristo' recently observed, "is like a five-hundred year old refectory oak table, weathered, matured, battered but unmistakably antique and completely irreplaceable."

"A King can create a nobleman, Gerald, but he can't create a 'gentleman.'
The whole cafe broke into cheers. The English gentleman had won another round!

I toasted the cheerful peasantry of Vaud!

'Well Spoken'

Gerald de Vaud asked me a question yesterday which profoundly embarrassed me.

"What does 'well spoken' mean?"

I didn't know which way to turn. Worse than being asked which class you belong to.

"Is it something to do with grammar or eloquence?"

"Never! Well..." I stammered, " it, well... you could call it RP, that is 'Received Pronunciation' or a 'standard' or a 'cultured' or a' cultivated' accent' or... well... upper class, private school, Eton, BBC, Oxbridge... you only have to listen to Parliamentary debates, the Tories, very obvious, very upper indeed."

"A fellow told me you Englishman are all socially 'branded on the tongue.' Is this true?"

"Only if you're lower class."

He also said it was impossible for an Englishman to open his mouth without making some other Englishman despise him."

"This chap you talked to, where did he come from?"

"Wales."

"That accounts for it. A malcontent. Welsh accent, you see, is the kiss of death, striking miners, peasants and poverty. Worse than being legless in a wheel chair. Cost Neil Kinnock, the old socialist leader, the last election. That accent put off, they reckon, at least 70% of the English electorate."

"What about Richard Burton, he was Welsh."

"But he went to Oxfords"

"What about the Scots?"

"Very business like. They've got their own national bank. They bashed us about. Not the Welsh. We bashed them about and they stayed bashed."

"Where did this BBC upper class accent come from?"

"The private schools of the 19th century, Eton, Harrow, carried forward by Oxbridge into this century. Enshrined by the BBC in the public ear when they first went on the air in 1922. Had to have a good accent. Before that only 7% of the populace ever heard the voices of their politicians."

"So you can never escape the tyranny of accent?"

"You don't have to escape if you're upper class."

"Is there a rule for knowing an upper class accent? "

"If you can detect what region the person comes from, then it's not an upper class accent."

"Why does it assume such importance?" . . . .

"Because an upper class accent is associated with, power, privilege, prestige, wealth, influence, the aristocracy, royalty. For example if a policeman approaches you, he'll treat you with much greater respect if you have an upper class accent Similarly in shops. Never know what contacts you have. And it's essential for promotion, interviews, getting to the top. Professors Honey and Crystal, both noted linguistics experts, have discovered in their researches that if you talk with an upper class accent, you are likely to be regarded as better looking, more intelligent and even cleaner!"

"Cleaner?"

"Well, you can always get a bath at your club, ha, ha!"

"Is there no way out of all this class?"

“Yes, you can take elocution lessons, but only in the right place. A fabulous elocutionist, one Mrs Cusforth of Cambrideg has helped at least twenty Cabinet Ministers to sound just right, that is, Tory, private school, upper class, even if they weren’t quite from the top drawer.”

“What is the difference in pronunciation? Give me an example, please.” ‘Well, ‘often’, the ‘t’ is pronounced by the lower orders, of’ten. But the upper classes pronounce it ‘offen. No ‘t’. There’s world of a difference. Tells you at once who’s upper, who’s lower.”

“And other words? Are they the same?”

“I can assure ‘you my, dear Gerald, every word in the Complete Oxford Dictionary is either upper class, middle class or lower class. The rest is academic. Fact of life.”

“What about the Australian accent or the Amercan or the South African?”

“They are unrelievedly hideous!”

“But, being over here, don’t you think you should learn a foreign language?”

“No. Everybody speaks English.”

“Perhaps you should make an effort.”

“Look, Gerald, if English was good enough for Jesus Christ and the twelve apostles, it’s good enough for me!”

What could Gerald say?

So we ordered another bottle.

Fair Profits for the House of Windsor

I joined my friend in the Valaisan wine celler in the centre of town. I was in a considerable state of agitation. I'd just returned from a visit to the UK.

"Gerald" I said, "last night I saw the nastiest TV programme I ever saw in my life." I paused painfully, "It said the House of Windsor was robbing the dead. Sorry! Not too upset are you? Want me to go on?"

"My friend" said Gerald, "I have always valued your amazingly frank confidences. Tell me more at once!"

"Are you sure? - some of it is pretty ugly."

"Do not spare the details, what else are friends for?"

"Quite right. Sorry again. Well, the Queen's got this Duchy of Lancaster, makes three million a year from it, tax free, perfectly entitled to, of course. Well, if you're a tenant on the estate and you die without making a will, the Queen can confiscate your estate. It's her right. It's ancient. I mean, they brought on this weeping woman who said the Queen had taken the entire estate of her life-long companion and wouldn't even let her have enough money for a tombstone for him."

"That is perfectly dreadful!" exclaimed Gerald.

"Sorry. I knew you'd be upset."

Gerald is a great humanist.

"How could they permit such invasions of royal privacy?! What else?"

"Well, you know our stupid Race Relations Act, where you have to give jobs to blacks? Well, the Queen is exempt from it. Common sense! Well, the Queen's also exempt from the Protection of Employees Act, so she can pay them what she likes. They can't appeal to a Wages Tribunal. Seems logical to me. And the Sex Discrimination Act, where you've got to appoint bloody women, she only employs four on her entire staff. She's exempt from that Act too. Thank God! Why not? Don't we, her faithful subjects, recognize she has lots of ancient rights even if we don't know exactly what they are. Why throw all this golden mystique to the public like a soiled rag?"

"What's the problem then?" . .

"This bloody programme said out loud it was all wrong! Even her private wealth!"

"No, not that!? Why?"

"God knows. Her private wealth is controlled by those magnificent City bankers, the Coutts, an old county family. But the Queen is also exempt from the Companies Act of 1985 so she doesn't have to disclose a penny. No shares, no holdings. Nothing public. She pays no tax anyway. No one knows how rich she is. Three, four, five billion, does it matter, it's hers! Her mystique again, her privilege, her right. Why, one commentator said there were more leaks from M16, England's counter espionage organization than from the Queen's financial operators. Such sarcasm. It was that sort of programme."

"But can't her employees tell all?"

"Never! They have to sign the Official Secrets Act! If anyone tells on Royalty, beware! I don't mean execution, but prison certainly. And all this about her private yacht, seventeen million for a re-fit! If it cost that, then she should have a new yacht! Her private aircraft and family trains make millions for the nation in good will alone. And so there's no records of all the private gifts to our royals! Records? Do you keep records of the gifts you received on your wedding day? So nobody knows the sum total of the crown jewels or works of art either, so what? Mystery! Half the pleasure of living under a monarchy. And this tragedy of the old Windsor fire. Of course the nation should have paid, out of respect alone, ungrateful wretches! So millions were out of work and going bankrupt. No excuse! And look at what the splendid little woman did, opened Buckingham Palace, her home! Only eighteen splendid rooms out of six hundred but already the gift shop is showing fantastic profits. Yes, there's still loads of love out there! Go to the Palace, Gerald, see the unique range of products: crown-shaped chocolates, first-day cover envelopes, head-scarves of royals. All so popular an American Firm got a Royal Warrant to sell under the banner of the House of Windsor, royal hand-made cushions, royal whisky tumblers, royal bookends, royal Wemyss Cats, royal silver thimbles, royal umbrellas and royal fragrances. Why, next year the Royal Yacht is going to market some of this refined merchandise in the Caribbean! Our Royals will make a laughing stock of the whole world, you'll see!"

"Laughing stock?' You may be right again this time."

"Cheers Sorry, last bit now. Kept the worst for last. Damn commentator quoted a 'George Orwell', some kind of renegade obviously, 'England is a family with the wrong members in control.' Such...perversion! Another traitor, the unspeakable Jeremy Flaxman TV, spewed up this gem, 'At the apex of British society the House of Windsor is the keystone that keeps the whole ghastly British class system in business."

"What?" asked Gerald, "did a true Brit really say that?"

"In 2003! Beyond belief! Drink up there, Gerald! Cheers! Pretty devastating, isn't it? Well, let me assure traitors Flaxman and Orwell here and now," I shouted out loud, "without the House of Windsor there would be no bloody business in Britain at all!" I drained my glass and slammed it down on the table.

"Thanks for listening, Gerald, I feel better now. Hope I didn't upset you. What do you think of it all?"

"I believe, my friend;' said Gerald, rather mysteriously I thought, "that your friendly Windsors are going to have to sell a hell of a lot of that ‘royal fragrance’ next year.”

Back to Republics

I looked at the picture of our gracious Queen on the bedroom wall of the clinic I had so sadly found myself in.

Gerald was sitting on a chair by the bed.

"I am not mad, " I said.

"Of course not," Gerald reassured me, "I've got the doctor's notes."

"Everything just exploded. Horrid memories!"

"Don't repress them. You've let nearly all of it hang out. Just that one word to go."

"I still can't say it, Gerald. And you, old friend, what you've had to bear all your life, words like 'commune' 'canton', 'referendum', and ugh!' 'confederation.' I take my hat off to you. And this 'R' thing, you've learned to live even with that Gerald, a braver comrade no man could have!"

"The 'R' word, then!"

I covered my ears.

"Frogs! Revolution! Guillotine! Yes..." I burst out, "but.... not on Bastille Day! Frogs, our Queen, 'greedy they said. 'Greedy'? Her! Bad enough.... but..."

"Shouldn't have got into a fight."

"Just saw red!"

"The final word now, the 'R' one, come on, my friend. Doctor, police waiting, nurses, entire staff. Come on or they'll keep you in here for a week! Now!"

I saluted the Queen, screamed "Republican!" and fell out of bed. Gerald dashed to the door.

"Quick! Black coffee!" he shouted to the nurses outside, "he's come to, got to keep him moving. Black coffee!"

They kept me walking in circles for hours, black coffee kept coming. The entire staff of doctors and nurses were all helping.

"Republican, republican, republican...." I recited until at last some of the terror of the word receded.

"Republican," I suddenly said firmly, looking straight at them. They all broke into cheers. I smiled wanly. Yes the snake had been laid.

"You can now leave," said Gerald, "the Police will give you a caution about insulting citizens of the French Republic on Bastille Day and you're a free man."

"I was only joking," I said, "and anyway they started it."

"Don't be too sure;' he cautioned.

Outside, after my release, faithful old Gerald continued my 'cure.'

"Say his name. Come on!"

"TT... Tom..... PPPaine!" I ejaculated.

"The greatest Englishman!"

"No, no, no, not that!"

"Face up to it! Say it!"

"The greatest Englishman!' There! I did it!"

"The Father of the French Republic."

"The Father of the French Republic!"

"The Father of the American Republic."

"The Father of the American Republic."

"He was an Englishman from Thetford in Norfolk."

"...was an Englishman from Thetford... in Norfolk!"

"The greatest Englishman!"

"The greatest Englishman!"

I'd got it all out.

"The Rights of Man by Tom Paine is one of the greatest republican documents the world has ever seen."

"The Rights of Man by Tom Paine is one of the greatest republican documents the world has ever seen!"

"You have come through! How does it feel, my friend?"

"Gerald, I feel... at liberty!"

"Know the truth and the truth shall set you free!"

"Yes,' I replied with fervour, "God save the Queen!"

"Shit!" muttered Gerald aside, "a relapse already."

But what had I said, I wondered?

"Epesses is the only cure. Come on!"

We were soon enjoying a bottle of 'the only cure,' an eternal joy well beyond mere republicans, I thought slyly.

Juxtaposition (1):

From the Hippolytus of Euripedes Hippolytus:

O Zeus, why did you house them in the light of day,
Women, man's evil, a false glittering counterfeit?
For if you wished to propagate the race of men,
This should not have been brought about by women's means.
Instead, men should have offered in exchange their wealth
Within your temples – gold or silver or a weight
Of bronze, and bought their children for the price they paid
Each at its proper value. And then they could live
In free and easy homes and have no need of wives.
This makes it clear how great an evil women is:
The father who breeds and educates one, pays a dowry too
That she may live elsewhere and he be free from pain.
And then the man who takes this curse within his house
Delights in adding fine adornments to her shape,
Worthless itself, to spend time in finding dresses for her,
The fool, and wastes away the substance of his house.
He's in a cleft stick; for, if he can marry well
And likes his new relations, then his wife will be
A bitter thing; and if his wife is good, he'll find
Worthless relations , bad and good luck counterpoised.
Easiest for him who has settled in his home a wife
Whose mind's a total blank, a simple useless thing.
I hate a clever woman, and in my house never would

Have one wiyh more ideas than women ought to have.
For Cyprus inculcates more often evil ways
Among the clever ones, whereas the helpless kind
Are barred from loose behavior by their lack of wit.
No servant ever should have access to a wife:
Their company should be some biting speechless beast,
So that they could not even speak to anyone,
Nor get an answer back from those whom they address.
But as it is, wives who are bad, make their bad plots
At home, and then their servants carry them outside.
Like you, you miserable wretch, who came to me
to make arrangements for my father's sacred bed.
With running water I shall wash my ears and wipe
away your words. How could I ever be so base,
I, who, just hearing you, must think myself unclean?
Be sure, what saves you woman, is my sense of right.
If carelessly , I had not bound myself by oaths,
For sure I would have told my father of all this.
And now, so long as Theseus is away from home,
I shall be absent too, and keep a silent tongue:
And then returning with my father, I shall watch
How you will meet his eye, you and your mistress too.
Yes, I shall know, having tasted of your shamelessness,
I would destroy you all, - never shall have enough
Of hating women, though they say that I'm always
saying the same thing. Women too are always bad.

Either let someone teach them to be self-controlled,
Or else allow me still to tread them under foot.

Translated by Rex Warner

Juxtaposition (1) contd:

"All women move me – old, young, tall, short, fat, thin, thick, heavy, light, beautiful, charming, living, dead. I also love cows, she-monkeys, sows, bitches, mares, hens, geese, turkey hens, lady hippos and mice. But the categories of female I prefer are wild beasts and dangerous reptiles. There are women loathe. I'd like to murder one or two or have myself killed by one of them. The world of women is my universe. It's the world I have developed in, perhaps, not for the best, but no man can really feels he knows himself if he detaches himself from it."

Ingmar Bergman, quoted by Francois Truffaut.

The Hermit Express

My father took out his favourite walking stick from the old 25 pounder brass shell-case standing in the hall. He had on his best tweed suit and brown trilby hat, the 'off duty' uniform of all true ex-army officers. He was going to catch the Express from West Wales, Carmarthen, to a royal meeting at Buckingham Palace, chaired by the Duke of Norfolk and then on to another at the College of Arms, in the City, presided over by Black Rod. (The wobbly bridge now stands opposite the noble genealogical pile overlooking the Thames.) My Dad was Wales Herald Extraordinary, which meant he was unpaid, except for a few expenses and one ducal banquet. We walked outside to the small front garden. Dad swished his cane in the air and pointed towards the station.

"By Express from Fishguard. Only one stop more, at Cardiff, then straight through," he said, "glad you could come, boy." He always called me 'boy' although I was twenty-nine.

My Mother hurried out of the front door carrying my father's small London suitcase with its socks, sandwiches, documents, diaries and royal minutes. My Mam always prepared Dad for the journey.

"Where's my half crowns?" Dad asked.

The 'half crowns' were Dad's working currency. They harked back to the time of Edward V11, a period my father was very comfortable with. He would often return home with the 'half-crowns' unspent and the sandwiches uneaten. But it was a warm, familiar routine which both enjoyed. Mam and Dad were the happiest couple I had ever known.

"Thank you again, my dear," he responded, kissed her and pocketed the money, uncounted. I embraced my Mam and with my father striding ahead, made for the familiar sounds of puffing steam engines and the sharp whistles of the Guards, ghosts now long vanished. My father made for a first-class compartment, his one luxury, on expenses, of course, a place, befitting a royal envoy, where he could go over his notes in peace. I leaned back in my plush, upholstered corner, my head resting on the starched antimacassar, another thing forever forgotten, and dozed off. I distantly recalled one of the many trips I had made with my Dad. He couldn't drive so I had the benefit of his genealogical expertise among the leaves of our family tree, and beyond. He always talked non-stop about the Jones tribe, and what a tribe - bankrupt butchers, illegitimate offspring by Catholic priests, runaway debtor wives, fugitives to the Pampas, illegal fornicators at Sunday School, never a dull moment! On that particular occasion, the first on the list to visit was my Uncle Madryn, my father's younger brother. I had seen him only once in my whole life.

"Don't expect him to come to the door,' my Dad had warned. I well remembered the single time I had viewed Madryn before, and I remember not because of what he said but because he had not said a word to me at all. He spoke only in Welsh and only to my father. My father seemed to have accepted this social arrangement in good part, so I followed suit. No problem. Just before he was forty, Madryn had made three startling changes in his life, my Dad explained to me – he got married, he bought a small holding-cum-cottage with his life's savings, and he changed his job. His new forty-four year old wife was a red-haired Irish widow, cheery in spite of her loss. The only distinctive thing about her speech was that it was terribly, terribly slow, yet she was no mute, especially in defence of her now beloved husband. As her dowry, she brought her aging sister, an irrecoverable alcoholic, to live with them. The thirsty one, like Madryn, lived on monosyllables and she only said her prayers out loud on Xmas Day after a good Christian binge. Madryn had vowed to take care of her till she passed on; and care he did, however drunk she might have been, with tenderness and affection till the day she died. Both sisters adored their constant guide and kindly protector, although all three were often speechless for months. The women hovered over him like the baby Jesus itself whenever he appeared. Apart from the various, sad vinous episodes, they managed to make it a bright household with lots of hope.

The old shepherd's cottage was set high above the last few houses of the village. It had been built into the rocky outcrops of the steep hillside. The tufted ground around was laced with rabbit tracks, scattered sheep droppings, all canopied with immense prickly yellow gorse. It was undoubtedly a place where one could get quickly lost. Behind the house ran a disguised pathway to the kitchen. Here there was a back door to nowhere. Once opened from the inside, all that could be seen were wild tangles of thick ivy strangling the rowan trees, climbing dodder in profusion, black bryony, and huge immemorial growths of prickly bushes blocking the way. The foliage and underbrush were carefully cultivated so no one could see the hidden pathway beneath, from inside or outside. It all seemed impenetrable. For Madryn, this was the exit route to his innumerable hideaways and bolt holes. Here he could embrace his silent, de-peopled, non-syllabic world. He had also made sure he had a good view from the windows and could spot a moving human five miles off. When he did, he would dash off to the door to nowhere, and leave his faithful flame-haired Palace guard to deal with the intruders. My uncle was soon established as the uncrowned hermit of that ancient hundred.

On the way home, after not gaining entry to the cottage, nor having a skirmish with the gallowglasses, I recalled asking my Dad why uncle Madryn wanted to be a hermit? My father's reply to me, still a boy, was memorable, "well, Madryn told me once – "because no one wants to talk to you and everyone leaves you alone - " seems reasonable enough to me,' - words which sank deep into my sub-conscious, words which I would constantly resurrect. The first time was a few days later, when I was with my father in the company of some of his friends. One of them finally noticed me standing there and decided to talk to me. He leaned down and asked me the inevitable question – "And what do you want to be when you're grown up?" A vision of Madryn flashed before my eyes, and I enthusiastically replied, "A hermit!" This was greeted with loud laughter and pretended disbelief, 'we grown ups," they protested, "we're not so bad, lad, you'll see!

"But why a hermit?" insisted the original joker.

Then I uttered the immortal words, "because no one talks to you and everyone leaves you alone!" This provoked further howls of fake protest and empty reassurances about adults, which as far as I was concerned, were the usual fabrications, laced with the completely insincere. I noticed my father smiling gently, he knew the source of my ripostes, and in his quiet way, approved of them. That utterance went down in the family annals and were trotted out on every festive occasion. I began smiling with my father, enjoying those shadowy, shared sentiments.

"Boy! Boy! Wake up!" Dad was shaking my shoulder. The train was slowing down. "Look, we're coming into Cardiff!"

I blinked myself awake as my father stationed himself at the door with his cane. As soon as the train stopped, my father leapt out, "Come on, boy!" he ordered, I kept up with him as he strode swiftly down to the head of the train. "Where are we going?! I asked. "A surprise," he replied mysteriously, and came to a halt by the massive cab of the hissing, puffing, looming iron horse. The door of the cab opened and a figure emerged, dressed in blue overalls and an official railway peaked cap. It was Madryn! So this is where he had ended up! He waved cheerfully to my father. He didn't seem to see me – a relief. It made me glad to see him. He clambered down and the two were soon in deep, animated conversation - in Welsh, of course. The exchanges seemed to be full of friendliness and brotherly affection. I wondered why they were being so urgent about it. Finally a whistle blast broke off the flow of words. The brothers paused, embraced each other, Madryn almost in tears, smiled through it all, for his tears were finally, I saw, tears of joy. He even waved in my direction. Although it was a vague gesture, it was enough. Father and I hurried back to our plush, posh first-class seats.

"What was that all about, Dad?" I asked.

"Well," he said settling down for a chat, "the three things Madryn did when he turned thirty-nine - I told you about them - well, they were worrying him like mad. He thought his marriage might be construed as a tactic to protect his privacy, frighten people off, and make the two women dependent on him for life so they would never leave him. I vehemently rejected this opinion and assured him, in addition, that drink was a side issue. I told him I had never seen such a happy couple, the sisters, I mean and he and his wife, too, and all were members of an exceptionally well adjusted little family, and that he had done a fine, upstanding thing to create it." I succeeded in reassuring him on that score. But he had developed doubts about the cottage itself, he was such a worrier, was that also just 'a private fortification to keep out the world,' 'a self-centred stratagem for himself '? I rejected that view vigorously too. I pointed out the positive benefits of the purchase, it was shared by all and sundry, whether they were seen or not – and that he had saved the antique shepherd's cottage as well as the young women, I emphasized that, especially his poor thirsty sister-in-law, and had given them a new life. True, he had opened up new vistas of silence for himself, but that was only to be expected from the head of a household! - all of which, I insisted, without exception, was an admirable thing. He was at once hugely relieved on that account too. Then as to his change of job – about dropping his milk rounds and becoming a top Express driver. He felt guilty about finding the best job in the world for himself, as senior driver on the whole line - an ideal situation, which meant being enclosed in a small mobile cell, without human company, without the necessity of speaking, which was impossible anyway because of the noise, all this was 'very heaven' to him, but was he, he asked, and he was as anxious here too, was he again guilty of the sin of selfishness? I assured him I had never seen him so unselfish or his cohabitees so sane and safe. And why, I ended with absolute certainty, look at your own brother here – how many brothers in the world have someone like you, you, my Madryn, my younger brother who succeeded so well in life he was able to drive his older brother all the way in a downright regal compartment to the very gates of Buckingham Palace itself - with the bonus of his best son at his side!?" Dad paused for breath, "and this exceptional conveyance of yours, brother Madryn, "he finished, "is called..." he looked at me with a raised eyebrow and his slow, amused, smile - "...the hermit Express!" I shouted out!

"Wait till your mother hears about this when we get home, boy!" he promised, and we both laughed all the way to Paddington Station - we really did!

Titles from Creative Print Publishing Ltd

Fiction

The Shadow Line & The Secret Sharer ISBN 978-0-9568535-0-9	Joseph Conrad
Kristina's Destiny ISBN 978-0-9568535-1-6	Diana Daneri
Andrew's Destiny ISBN 978-0-9568535-2-3	Diana Daneri
To Hold A Storm ISBN 978-0-9568535-3-0	Chris Green
Ten Best Short Stories of 2011 ISBN 978-0-9568535-5-4	Various
The Lincoln Letter ISBN 978-0-9568535-4-7	Gretchen Elhassani
Dying to Live ISBN 978-0-9568535-7-8	Katie L. Thompson
Keeping Karma ISBN 978-0-9568535-6-1	Louise Reid
Escape to the Country ISBN 978-0-9568535-8-5	Patsy Collins
Lindsey's Destiny ISBN 978-0-9568535-9-2	Diana Daneri
RELICK ISBN 978-1-909049-03-1	Steven Gepp
It Hides In Darkness ISBN 978-1-909049-04-8	Ross C. Hamilton
Transmission of Evil ISBN 978-1-909049-06-2	Mandy Sheering
Ransom ISBN 978-1-909049-07-9	Don Nixon
Milwaukee Deep ISBN 978-1-909049-05-5	G. Michael

PANDORA ISBN 978-1-909049-09-3	Marcus Woolcott
Alaric, Child Of The Goths ISBN 978-1-909049-08-6	Daniel F. Bowman
For Catherine ISBN 978-1-909049-01-7	Elizabeth Morgan
ANGELS UNAWARES ISBN 978-1-909049-02-4	Dedwydd Jones
Black Book on the Welsh Theatre ISBN 978-1-909049-11-6	Dedwydd Jones
MASKS or The Golden Omega ISBN 978-1-909049-13-0	Dedwydd Jones
Hilarious Tales For Kids and Grown Ups ISBN 978-1-909049-15-4	Dedwydd Jones
The Man in the Scottish Lunatic Asylum ISBN 978-1-909049-25-3	Dedwydd Jones
SLADE All In Black and White ISBN 978-1-909049-26-0	Pam Edwards
Blackbird and the Dove ISBN 978-1-909049-28-4	Gary Dawson
The Man From Marsden ISBN 978-1-909049-27-7	Chris Bedford

NonFiction

Amazonia – My Journey Into The Unknown ISBN 978-1-909049-00-0	Adam Wikierski
Recollections of Pathos and the Greek Islands ISBN 978-1-909049-12-3	Les Burgess

Contacting Creative Print Publishing Ltd

Creative Print Publishing are publishers of books covering various genres including all kinds of fiction, non-fiction and life histories.

For more details contact:

Creative Print Publishing Ltd
office Suite 8 & 9
Heritage Exchange Business Centre
South Lane Mills
South Lane
Elland
HX5 0HQ

United Kingdom

Web: http://www.creativeprintpublishing.com

Email: info@creativeprintpublishing.com Tel:

+44 (0) 1484 314 985

Lightning Source UK Ltd.
Milton Keynes UK
UKOW04f1426111014

239968UK00002B/16/P

9 781909 049291